© OVERSEAS MISSIONARY FELLOWSHIP

First published 1980

ISBN 0 85363 133 6

Published by Overseas Missionary Fellowship,
Belmont, The Vine, Sevenoaks, Kent, TN13 3TZ, UK

Typeset by Bookmag, Inverness.

CONTENTS

Introduction	3
East meets west	8
Work out your own salvation	12
The first 150 years	18
How it's done	26
Central Thailand	38
South Thailand	64
Bangkok	72
North Thailand	78
Into the future	99

INTRODUCTION

In 1828 the first Protestant missionaries arrived in Thailand. In 1978 the Protestant churches in Thailand joined together to celebrate in worship and praise to the Lord for 150 years of Protestant work. In that same year, 1978, the Maitri chit Church in Bangkok, founded in 1837 and the oldest indigenous Chinese Protestant church in the Far East, sent out its first missionaries around the Kingdom of Thailand.

What have these 150 years to show? A small church numbering approximately 45,000 out of a population of 45 million seems small fruit indeed after so many years of missionary endeavour. Nor have these results been achieved cheaply and without cost and sacrifice. To walk through the Protestant cemetery in Bangkok is to read the history of the Christian church from those who, beginning with pioneers Tomlin and Gutzlaff, have come, laboured and laid down their lives for the Lord's sake and the Gospel. Nor is Thailand church history and OMF history written only in the cemetery of Bangkok. In South Thailand and North Thailand the same story can be seen, of OMF missionaries coming to this resistant land and laying down their lives in order to lay the foundation of the Church of Jesus Christ.

The land of Thailand consists of many different ethnic groups. OMF missionaries, true to the pioneer spirit which led to China and from China to the countries of Southeast Asia, can be found not only working with the ethnic Thai but with minority groups throughout Thailand. In North Thailand we work with the Yao, Hmong, Akha, Lisu and Karen tribal people and with the Shan. In South Thailand the Gospel is taken to the Thai and especially to the Malay people who comprise 80% of the population in those four southern provinces.

In 1951 when OMF first came to Thailand they agreed to work in areas and among people where there was no other Christian work or witness. The pervading attitude amongst missionaries then was one of a deep sense of urgency. Impelled by the experience of Communist takeover in China, they were driven by an acute sense of the possible shortness of time available for work in Thailand; they were driven also by a deep passion for the lost in Thailand as they faced the vast numbers of unreached Thai and tribal people, as well as the resistant Malays in the south. This burning urgency had a two-fold effect upon the strategy at that time. The first was the aim to reach as wide an area of population as possible in the shortest space of time, by placing missionaries far and wide throughout Central Thailand in order to occupy the provincial capitals in that area. The second effect of the urgency was a major emphasis on the distribution of literature on as wide a scale as possible. 'The present strategy' wrote someone at that time, 'is one of preparation of the soil by prayer, widespread seed sowing in the form of Gospel sales, and broadcast tract distribution.'

How good the Lord has been! Today there is a church in these areas, and a light has been lit that shall never be extinguished. From those early beginnings the Lord has opened up wider and wider opportunities, so that today there are something like 260 OMF missionaries involved in tribal evangelism and church planting, Bible translation and literacy, leadership training, agricultural work, all helping to establish churches amongst the tribal people in the north. Today the Gospel is reaching Thai in Central Thailand, Bangkok and South

Thailand through rural and urban church planting, Bible teaching, leadership training, Bible schools, through medical work, student work, literature, camps and children's work, in fact by all means possible. The Gospel is reaching the fiercely resistant Malay through hospital work and leprosy clinics, through evangelism, personal work, village evangelism and persistent presentation of the Truth. In all cases, men, women and children are being won to the Lord and slowly but surely the Temple of God is being erected as living stone is placed upon living stone.

For many years the Kingdom of Siam (as it was known) remained an exotic but largely unknown country squeezed between Burma and Indo-China. A country which has never been colonized, though its neighbours had, it tended to remain quietly unknown, content to continue as a land of smiles and enigmatic obscurity. Today things have changed dramatically. The fall of Indo-China and the flood of refugees who have poured across Thailand's borders, calling forth world shock and pity, have thrust this country into the limelight of world attention. The political balance of power in Southeast Asia, the agonies of war in Indo-China, the harrowing state of affairs that is Kampuchea, have thrust upon Thailand the inescapable attention of the world and a role to play which means it can no longer go quietly about its own business. In the spiritual realm, at the same time, the worldwide prayer thrust for Thailand in 1978-79 has generated an interest and burden for this country and a concern for the Lord to break through in power and glory here. Nor has this interest and attention lessened. Who can forget that in the last five years sixteen OMF missionaries and their children and friends have died because of their commitment to Christ to bring the Gospel to this country.

This book, therefore, is concerned to tell the story of the OMF in Thailand. It is concerned to give a proper understanding of the country, its culture and religion, which will help to show the barriers of resistance that have been erected to the Gospel and the ways in which these walls of resistance can be brought down. At present OMF work is organised into four different administrative fields on a geographical and sociological basis, so the chapters which follow are also divided in this way. Yet the principles remain the same. If church growth is to take place, then there are principles which can apply equally wherever and with whoever we are working.

For 27 years we have sought to plant the Church of the Lord Jesus Christ in this country. For the last two years there has been a call for special prayer for breakthrough. This book tells how the break-in into the enemy's territory to spoil his goods began. Breakthrough, that ingathering harvest for Christ of the many, is what we continue to long, pray and labour for.

David Pickard
(Area Director for Thailand)
January 1980

TOWARDS NEW LIFE

1555	First RC priests in Thailand
1819	Catechism and tract printed in Thai (in India)

Beginnings 1828—1851

1828	First Protestant missionaries — Gutzlaff and Tomlin
1835	Arrival of Dr D B Bradley — pioneered Christian medical work and printing
1837	Maitri Chit Baptist Church established in Bangkok — oldest indigenous Protestant church in the Far East.
1840	Presbyterian missionaries arrived—continuously at work till the present day.

Struggles 1851—1884

1851	King Mongkut becomes king—begins modernization of Thailand
1858	Arrival of Dr Daniel McGilvray
1859	First Presbyterian convert baptized—after 19 years.
1878	King Chulalongkorn pronounces Edict of Religious Toleration

Growth 1884—1914

During this period the Northern Thai church grew from 150 to 7,000.

Arrested growth 1914—1940

Growth rate down to 0.7% per annum through lack of shepherding, emphasis on institutions.

1929	Christian and Missionary Alliance begin work in Thailand.
1938—39	Revival through ministry of John Sung

Testing 1941—1945

Second world war. Japanese occupation. Many turned back.

Recovery and Growth 1946—1978

1947	WEC arrive
1949	Southern Baptists arrive
1951	New Tribes Mission arrive
1951	OMF arrive
1953	Marburger Mission arrive
1970—1973	Revival in North Thailand
1970	Evangelical Fellowship of Thailand organised First All-Thailand Congress on Evangelism
1978	Celebration of 150th Anniversary of commencement of Protestant work. Second All-Thailand Congress on Evangelism

THAILAND AND HER NEIGHBOURS

OMF MILESTONES

Year	Milestone
1951	First OMF missionaries arrived in Thailand
1952	Work begun in Central Thailand and among the Yao in North Thailand
1953	OMF missionaries resident in 8 provinces of Central Thailand. Work begun in South Thailand
1954	Clinics opened in Wiset and Inburi, Central Thailand. First baptisms in Paknampho, Central Thailand. Work begun among the Akha, Meo, Pwo Karen
1955	Saiburi clinic opened. Mr Arphon and Mr Samyong converted.
1956	Manorom hospital opened
1957	First baptisms in Yala, South Thailand, and first Yao baptised in North
1959	First believers conference in Yala
1960	Saiburi hospital opened
1963	Leprosy treatment programme started in South Thailand
1966	Dry Season Evangelism in Central Thailand organized for first time, using films, teams of students. Phayao Bible Training Centre opened
1968	Nongbua hospital opened
1969	Makasan hostel opened in Bangkok
1970	First baptism of Lisu in Thailand. Cassettophones introduced for teaching isolated Christians. 'Thai Christian Students' founded
1971	Bangkok Bible College opened
1972	Makasan Church, Bangkok, started
1973	First Muslim converts baptized in South Thailand
1974	Suan Plu Church, Bangkok, started
1975	Translation of New Testament in Meo completed. Missionaries withdrawn from Vietnam, Cambodia and Laos. Dyke road built at Manorom to prevent flooding.
1976	Programme of open-air film evangelism among Malays
1977	Thai Home Missions Board formed. Work begun among Sgaw Karen
1978	Road accident at Manorom — 12 killed. 'Towards New Life' evangelistic campaigns

EAST MEETS WEST

Thailand is a country 'on the go'. Everyone seems to be travelling. Ten-wheel trucks converge on Bangkok with their loads. Large orange Mercedes-Benz buses rush passengers at break-neck speed to every provincial town, while blue and silver air-conditioned buses take travellers in more comfort and ease. Pick-up trucks, converted to carry twenty or more people, penetrate to the smaller villages. In the towns, samlor drivers crowd their three-wheeled cycles around every arriving bus, vieing to take the travellers to their homes. Motorcycles have become the status symbol of teachers and local government officials, speeding to their schools and offices.

Side by side are the rich and the very poor. Scrawny cows and buffalos eat what grass they can find from the dry brown fields, while nearby a progressive farmer is planting out his second crop of rice, with the help of water pump and tractor. Modern heart surgery is performed in the quiet, efficient hospitals of the capital, while thousands in those same Bangkok streets or in the villages throughout the country still go to the spirit doctor with his charms, sacred strings, taboos and magic chants blown over the sick person.

Bangkok is a thriving business centre. Japanese consumer goods fill the shops along with products from the West. Women in the luxury hotels wear the latest Paris fashions and tourists from Frankfurt and Tokyo, Chicago, Sydney and Singapore are graciously received in the quiet, gentle way of the Thai.

How is it that western ideas have been so widely accepted into education, medicine, travel and business, yet traditional ways of healing, of leadership and the age-old concepts of spirits and ghosts have remained, almost unaffected by the onrush of the 20th Century? Why is it that Japanese radios, TVs and cars are found everywhere, western films and TV programmes are watched by millions, yet the Gospel message has been received by only a fraction of one percent of the people?

Like many other developing countries, Thailand has tried to accept the good things of the West, but resist what it has judged as harmful. It wants to maintain its uniqueness, its political and cultural identity. It has tried — and largely succeeded — in 'containing' the effects of the West upon its institutions, values and cultural patterns. In his book on Thailand, Norman Jacobs says that the Thai react violently against anything that causes separation. They view 'separation' as the first step towards disunity and rebellion. One can see this in the way that Brahminism and Buddhism have been added onto, and fused into one with Animism, the fear of spirits. It is hard for many Thai to say to which of the three any particular ceremony belongs.

Christianity, however, is seen as a way of life that emphasizes separation. The Bible teaches that the Christian should not be involved in wrong-doing, he should separate from immorality. And the Gospel cannot mix with the doctrines and practices of other religions. Many do not realize that the power of Christ in an individual actually increases his concern for his neighbour. To become a Christian makes one a more responsible member of the community, more respectful to leaders and government.

'Cool-heart' country

The new arrival in Thailand quickly adapts to such practices as removing one's shoes before entering a house, and greeting people with the traditional 'wai' (the hands are put together in a praying position and the head bowed slightly). New missionaries must remember that the Thai attach great respect to the head, so one must never touch or point to anyone's head. Similarly, the feet are considered low and only referred to after a suitable 'excuse me'. When one needs to cross a room in front of other people, the head should be kept lower than other people's heads, which isn't very easy for tall Westerners.

'Attitudes' and 'standards' are harder to learn and adapt to, yet are so important for the missionary to learn if he is going to proclaim the Gospel of grace faithfully without giving offence. The Thai value patience and graciousness in the way a person walks, speaks and acts. The foreign guest can do immeasurable harm if he appears to be in a hurry, or raises his voice or acts in an impatient way.

Thai people have a strong sense of respect for their elders and those in positions of authority. In English, the words 'brother' and 'sister' differentiate the sex of the person, but in Thai the equivalent words differentiate by age, so that they mean 'elder' and 'younger' (brother or sister). The older person is accepted as having more 'merit' and therefore being worthy of respect. The village headman, district officer, head of police, provincial governor and King are given respect to a proportionately greater degree. Simple village folk bring presents of flowers, fruit or eggs when the provincial governor or other similar official comes to visit their village. And they respectfully sit on the ground and listen to his speech. They would not expect to ask a question or interrupt, since he is a 'noble one.'

Closely related to this is the avoidance of conflict. The 'cool heart' is valued as the highest virtue and Thai children are taught to remain calm in all circumstances and to avoid any display of emotion. It is considered wrong to shed tears at the funeral of a loved one. Such feelings are to be repressed and the ideal of 'detachment' is aimed at. This characteristic has been called the Thai 'social cosmetic' and is also seen in their politeness to strangers and visitors.

The Thai have been called 'opportunists' and they will often act out of self-interest, choosing the path that pleases or brings most advantage to the individual. Buddhism teaches that 'Every person must trust only in himself,' and children are encouraged to exercise their independence. Yet, the Thai hold in tension with this their dependence on others in their family and village community.

While marital faithfulness is viewed as right, young men are expected to 'have a fling' before they settle to the responsibilities of married life. It is also accepted as something regrettable but not too serious if a husband drifts into loose living. He may give this a measure of respectability by taking a 'minor wife' or just 'go for an outing' regularly. The wife will find her fulfilment in her children and family responsibilities and accept her husband's behaviour as unavoidable, though divorce is by no means uncommon.

Never lose face

Outward appearances are extremely important to a Thai. He has grown up to understand that a person is how he acts, and that he is what he is today as a result of how he lived in previous existences. Shop assistants in the large western-style department stores in Bangkok look extremely neat in their fashionable

clothes and make-up. Yet they sense no inconsistency when they leave their homes and walk past piles of refuse outside in the road or thrown out of the kitchen window.

Similarly, actions are not judged by the categories of 'right' and 'wrong' but rather by whether they cause shame or not. Children are scolded because their behaviour or rude speech might be seen or heard by others and so bring shame on the family. In order to avoid direct confrontation with the possibility of open disagreement, it is usual to have a 'middleman' in such delicate negotiations as arranging a marriage or sorting out marital problems. The middleman is able to absorb the emotions of each side and good outward appearances are thereby maintained.

The Thai are a fun-loving people and events and things are measured by their 'enjoyment'. One of the first phrases the new missionary learns and soon recognizes in conversation is 'mai pen rai' (never mind, it doesn't matter). The Thai have been called 'masters of unconcern'. If something can't be done today, never mind, we'll try again tomorrow. However, it should not be thought that the Thai cannot work hard or are lazy. When necessary, they can exert themselves and work long hours. Planting out rice seedlings can be back-breaking work and they stick at it under the blazing sun for eight or more hours a day.

There is a strong sense of fatalism in the mind of the Thai. The teaching of Buddhism has permeated his thinking to the extent that he views himself as an actor in a play, with the script all written long before. Life is like a wheel: each revolution represents one life spent on earth. We are born, grow up, get old and die. But the forces of our actions and desires carry us over into the next revolution — another life here on earth. Good actions in a previous existence cause happiness and good social position in this life. Bad actions cause unhappiness, sickness, accidents and birth into a poor family. It is not uncommon for people to shrug their shoulders after a bad road accident and say: 'It was their karma- the inevitable result of their actions in a previous life.'

QUESTIONS
1. What effect do you think increasing western influence (eg films, TV programmes etc) will have on the traditional Thai way of life?
2. Thai people try to hide what they really feel (by eg. not crying at funerals). How can a new missionary get to know the ways and culture of another country?
3. How would you help the relatives of a Thai person killed in a car accident?

WORK OUT YOUR OWN SALVATION

One of the main tourist attractions of Thailand is the Buddhist temples. Tourists in their thousands flock to see the Marble Temple, the Temple of the Emerald Buddha, the Temple of the Reclining Buddha and many others. Altogether, there are nearly 26,000 temples in the whole of Thailand and many of them are architecturally outstanding, with beautiful friezes or painted walls, depicting events from the life of Gautama Buddha. The temple is the social centre of the ordinary Thai village. In former days it was the school, town hall, hotel and bank as well as place of worship. Many of these functions have now been superceded, but the annual festival each temple holds to raise money continues to be one of the main sources of entertainment in rural areas. Films, plays, music and dancing are used as the attraction to get people along.

About 94% of the population of Thailand are Buddhists. Another 4% are Muslims, 1.3% are Confucians and approximately 0.5% are Christians (Protestant and Catholic). Most of the tribal people in the north are animists. The Buddhism followed in Thailand is Theravada or 'lesser Vehicle' which Buddhists consider to be closest to the writings of the Pali Scriptures. These were written some three centuries after the death of Buddha. It was in the 13th Century AD that monks from Sri Lanka brought Buddhism to Thailand and King Ram Kham Haeng invited them to reside in Sukhothai (the capital then) to spread their teaching. So that Buddhism began to take root and be absorbed into the local animistic religion.

Buddhism has had a very deep influence on the culture and thinking of Thai people. Dates follow the 'Buddhist Era' eg. 1980 AD = 2523 BE. Many public holidays are Buddhist holy days and fresh meat is not sold on the four holy days of the lunar month. School children are normally required to pay homage to Buddha each morning before the beginning of lessons, and most local Government offices have their own Buddhist shrine, where civil servants are expected to pay respect. Most private cars, buses and lorries have Buddhist pictures and symbols over the driver's seat as a means of protection. Drivers and passengers will put their hands together in respect to shrines as they drive past.

Buddhism has become very closely integrated with Thai nationalism. The three concepts of 'The Nation, Religion and the Monarchy' are currently being stressed to hold the people together and as a safeguard against Communism. To be a Thai is to be a Buddhist. According to the Constitution the King must be a Buddhist, and since the Thai revere their Royal Family so highly, anyone who changes his religion is looked on almost as a traitor.

Christianity is considered not only a 'foreign' religion but also inferior to Buddhism, because Christ was born 543 years after Buddha and also because what they have seen of western morals (in films and the behaviour of American military personnel and

some tourists) seems definitely inferior to their own standards.

To the Buddhist, the world is seen as a place of suffering and sadness. Gautama Buddha struggled with the problem of suffering until he experienced 'enlightenment', in understanding that the answer was to extinguish one's desires and thereby become immune to suffering. The ultimate goal is to break free from the cycle of death and rebirths and to enter 'Nirvana' — the complete extinction of consciousness. But very few Buddhists really hope to achieve Nirvana. If only they can be better off next time they are born, this is as high as their aspirations go.

Buddhists do not believe in a personal God and they have no answer to how the world began. Indeed, the word 'God' can mean the King, an idol, a revered priest, or a mythological angelic being. There is no 'Saviour' and the very idea that one person might die to save another is both meaningless and abhorrent to the Buddhist. One of their mottos is: 'Each person must trust only in himself' and the last recorded words of Buddha are: 'Work out your own salvation with diligence.' In order to be reborn 'higher up the scale' the Buddhist makes merit, believing that 'merit' will balance off his misdeeds. The main ways of merit-making are through performing prescribed religious ceremonies. A Buddhist is always supposed to be merciful and kind to others, but there is no specific merit-value attached to helping the poor, visiting the sick, or being honest and upright in daily living.

By far the most common way of making merit is by offering food to the priests. Rice and curry is spooned into their large bowls as the priests pass the homes between six and seven o'clock in the morning. The priests receive the food without any indication of thanks. It is the person giving who is thankful to the priest for the opportunity to make merit, and any thanks given by the priest would take away the merit from the offerer.

The next most common way is by entering the priesthood. This can be done for almost any length of time — a few days, the three months of the Buddhist 'Lent' or for a number of years. There is no shame in leaving the priesthood, nor is any great pressure exerted on the priests to remain in the priesthood for prolonged periods. Merit is not only accrued by the man himself, but also by his parents, particularly his mother who brought him into the world. In order to enter the priesthood, no period of study or preparation is needed. The only requirements are for the man to be at least twenty years of age, have his parents' agreement, not be in debt, an epileptic, nor have any infectious disease. Becoming a priest puts a man into a different category from other people. He enters the class of 'mana filled' people, which includes the king, other priests, images of Buddha and other sacred objects. For this reason, even the parents of a man in the priesthood bow down to him, because he has entered a higher level of existence.

Other ways of making merit are building or repairing temples, giving robes or other gifts to priests, attending a temple service on a holy day, and placing gold leaf on an image of the Buddha.

There are several different approaches to Buddhism in Thailand. Some stress meditation and self-discipline, in reaction against the preoccupation with merit-making that they see having been taken to extremes by many. Great interest has developed in recent years in amulets and charms, and there are now several monthly magazines in circulation that deal exclusively with these. Hospitals and charities will produce Buddhas or medallions as a means of raising funds.

The biggest event in a Thai person's life is his funeral! 'King Chulalongkorn Day' is on the anniversary of his death, not his birth. Some Thai (especially those from a Chinese background) want to know what kind of a funeral they would have before they decide whether to become Christians. Thai will talk as freely about what they want at their funeral as people in the West might talk about what kind of a wedding they want. The ultimate achievement is to have the King as the sponsor of one's cremation ceremony. Of course, Buddhist funeral ceremonies are filled with opportunities to make merit, such as feeding the priests, giving them new robes and listening to the chanting of sacred scriptures.

Buddhists believe that at death one's soul (which they understand to mean one's 'consciousness') may go to various levels of hell, in order to suffer for particularly bad things done in the life just over. Following this, one then passes through various levels of the twenty heavens before returning for the next 'life'. Buddha was illuminated after 500 such existences. It can be seen that heaven and hell are conceived of as only temporary and there-

fore robbed of much of their meaning. The Buddhist does not fear hell, nor does he greatly desire to go to heaven.

Demi-gods are believed to live in the higher levels of 'heaven' but they are capable of sin; they marry and exist in a form of life not unlike earthly existence. As a reaction to this, many Buddhists in Thailand today speak of 'heaven' and 'hell' as being simply states of mind in one's thoughts — much like 'pleasure' and 'remorse'. This only shows the uncertainty the Buddhist has about the 'after life'. In fact, he holds that anything outside this world is unknown and unknowable, the 'other world'. Yet he goes on to state that this 'other world' is in fact the only *real* world and that the physical world is a world of ignorance and illusion. Priests and those who seek to advance in their religion therefore try to detach themselves from this world of sensation and feeling, concentrating on the moral world that underlies it.

This 'other world' has to do with the judgement of right and wrong as decided by the law of 'karma'. 'Karma' literally means 'that which we have done', and includes both good and bad. But it is normally the bad karma that Buddhists are concerned with. The things we have done in a previous existence determine the level at which we now live. A good position in life, wealth, power, good health and beauty are considered to be indications that the person has stored up large amounts of merit in previous existences. But one is never sure when one's stock of merit will run out, so the wise person still keeps making more merit.

Brahminism

Buddhist beliefs and practices are mainly aimed at trying to obtain a better reincarnation in the next 'life'. Other beliefs and practices are aimed at helping meet the problems of this present life: thus the Thai try to weave together the beliefs and practices of Animism, Brahminism and Buddhism, according to their view of the world they live in. Brahminism was practised in India at the time of Buddha and it was from this religion that Buddhism grew. Marriage ceremonies follow a Brahmin ritual, as does the New Year Festival in April, which is believed to produce rain and ensure fertility of the ground. The annual ploughing ceremony and the blessing of seed beds are also from this source. There are ceremonies for raising the first post of a new house and blessing the house before people take up residence, and celebrations after good success, such as recovery from illness, the winning of a lottery prize etc. Brahminism also gives rise to fortune-telling using astrological divination. Young people consult the fortune-teller to know whether they will pass their exams and whom they will marry. The date (and even the time) for weddings, funerals, house building and making a journey are all fixed by the astrologer.

Animism

The fear of spirits is almost universal in Thailand, though there is divergence of opinion as to just what a spirit is. They are conceived of as being the ghosts of dead people, demons, and resident spirits of a plot of land, river, mountain or tree. Small 'spirit houses' by the side of the road at places where an accident has occurred are very common and almost every house in Thailand has its own 'spirit house'. Although these spirits are usually thought of as bad, to be feared and propitiated by offerings, they are sometimes thought to be benevolent and their help sought for protection or healing of illnesses.

Spirits are believed to be capable of causing sickness, bad dreams, madness or death and they can haunt houses or possess and control people.

Various supernatural objects are used as a protection against the effects of spirits. Buddhist images and other charms are worn around the neck or the waist, or may be inserted under the skin. These are believed to protect from danger and illness. Many soldiers wear charms which they believe prevent bullets from entering their body. Others are used to cause members of the opposite sex to be attracted to the wearer. Sacred texts are also recited over the sick, using water or candle smoke to 'blow' the words on to the patient.

This then is the background, the normal thinking of most Thai people. No conception of an Almighty, personal God who created the world; no clear understanding of what sin is and therefore their need of a Saviour; believing that no one can help them and that only their own good works can enable them to be reborn at a higher level in their next existence; surrounded by images of Buddha, offering food to the priests each morning for as long as they can remember— how great is their need to know the Good News of Salvation through our Lord Jesus Christ!

QUESTIONS

1. The Thai Buddhist uses words like 'God', 'sin', 'heaven' and 'hell' with an entirely different meaning from the Christian. What difficulties will this make for the evangelist? How can he overcome them?
2. How would you answer a Thai who says, 'All religions teach me to be good. Christianity and Buddhism are the same.'
3. 'To be a Thai is to be a Buddhist'. How can the missionary explain that becoming a Christian should make one a more responsible member of the community?
4. What Scripture verses would you use to answer the Buddhist concepts of reincarnation and karma? How would you explain what heaven and hell are really like?
5. Fear of spirits leads to the control of the mind and will by demonic powers. How are people thus controlled to be delivered?

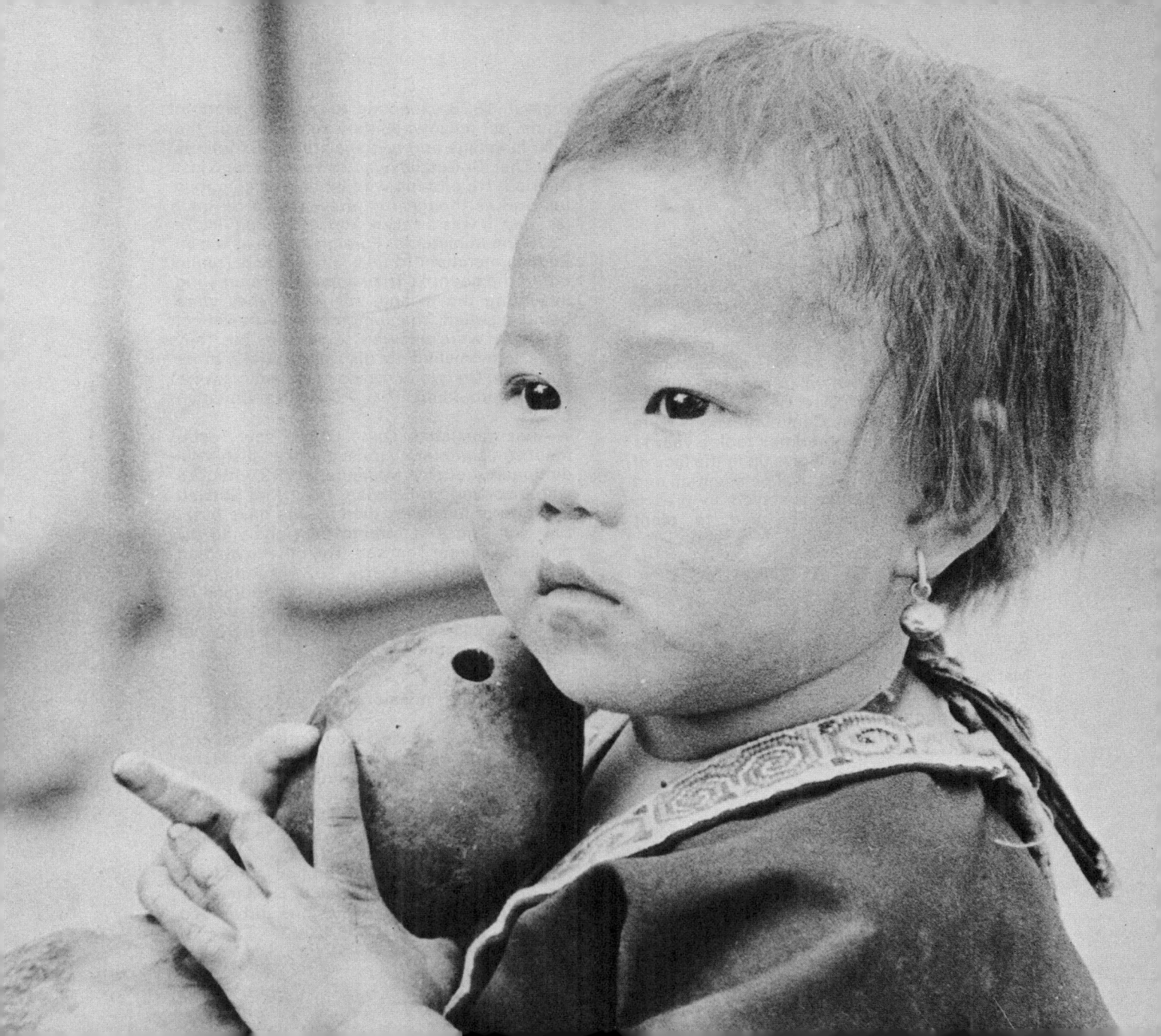

THE FIRST 150 YEARS

The command of Christ to proclaim the Gospel burned in the hearts of the early missionaries to Thailand. They had a biblical vision of men lost in sin and the great unfinished task of reaching the nations for God. They longed to share the good news of redemption which Jesus won for all men whatever race, colour, creed or language. Dire illness and great loneliness faced them. Communications were only by mail which sometimes took a year to reach them. They did not give up in the face of religious opposition, political persecution and criticism. These pioneers stayed to preach Christ, to make disciples and to plant churches.

THE PERIOD OF BEGINNINGS (1828-1851)

Before Protestant missionaries ever reached Thailand, Ann Judson had translated Matthew's Gospel, the catechism and a tract into Thai through meeting Thai prisoners of war in Rangoon, Burma. The Gospel was lost but the other two were printed in India in 1819.

Gutzlaff and Tomlin

The first Protestant missionaries in Thailand were a German, Dr Karl Gutzlaff, formerly of the Netherlands Missionary Society but by then independent, and Mr Jacob Tomlin of the London Missionary Society, They reached Siam in 1828 expecting to go on to work in China, but meanwhile they began to learn the Thai language and to translate the Scriptures into Thai. Dr Gutzlaff was 25 years old and just married. He and his wife worked desperately for God as though tomorrow would be their last day. It was a severe and costly conflict. In 1829 the Minister for Foreign Affairs asked an English merchant to take Gutzlaff and Tomlin out of the country. They appealed, requesting in writing the reasons for which they were being expelled. This remonstrance took effect and they were allowed to remain, but they were admonished to distribute books more sparingly. On two occasions royal edicts were issued forbidding Thai to receive Christian books.

After translating some of the New Testament and completing most of the English-Thai dictionary, both left by January 1832 without a single convert. In February 1831 Mrs Gutzlaff and one of her twins died as she gave birth. She was the first foreign missionary to lay down her life on Thai soil. The other twin died at four months old. (By 1927 another 49 missionaries had died, plus many children.) Dr Gutzlaff himself was broken in health, too weak to walk, so that friends had to help him onto a junk bound for China.

Early American missionaries

The American Baptists began work in Thailand in 1833, and in 1837 established the Maitri Chit Baptist Church in Bangkok. This is the oldest indigenous Protestant church in the Far East. They majored on the Chinese but a few Thai were also won to the Lord. The Mission withdrew in 1893.

The revival under Charles Finney in the USA brought Dr Dan Beach Bradley to Thailand. He had dedicated himself to missions and arrived in 1835. Ten days later he received a request in the name of the King to visit a company of slaves and captives ill with smallpox and cholera. He opened a small dispensary and treated about 100 patients daily, most of them Chinese, giving them Bible verses along with their prescriptions. Dr Bradley brought with him the first printing press to be used in the country, on which were printed not only portions of Scripture and tracts, but also the first government document ever printed (contrabanding opium). Mrs Bradley opened the first school for girls in 1836. Dr Bradley introduced successful innoculation against smallpox and performed the first surgical operation in the country. Later another missionary, Dr House, was the first to use ether anaesthetic in an operation on a Buddhist priest. Others established the first permanent hospital (1882) and the first systematic treatment of leprosy.

The Presbyterians

The Presbyterian Board of Foreign Missions has been working in Thailand continuously from 1840 until the present day. Like the other missions they met many barriers at first, such as an anti-foreign king, some opposing Buddhist priests and rampant disease — in 1849 an estimated 35,000 died of cholera in Bangkok. It was 19 years before they baptized their first convert.

From 1845 onwards missionary Jesse Caswell taught English and Science to HRH Prince Mongkut, then a Buddhist abbot. Caswell died in 1848, and in 1851 Prince Mongkut became king. That year he invited three women missionaries to teach English to women of the palace. During his reign King Mongkut introduced many western innovations which led to the modernization of Thailand. In this climate of change schools and hospitals became a main focus of mission work, taking up more personnel and finance. Many of the church leaders and evangelists became employed in these institutions, and initiative to reach out with the Gospel to the whole population was largely lacking. Although these fine Christian schools and hospitals created much goodwill and a climate of acceptability for missionaries, as well as helping to retain many of the children of Christians trained in them, they failed to make an appreciable impact in planting the church among the non-Christian population.

PERIOD OF STRUGGLE (1852-1883)

Life was not easy for the early Thai Christians. In 1850 four convert teachers were jailed for being in the employ of missionaries. The year before, eight Roman Catholic priests were banished from the country because they did not comply with the government order to turn their animals over to the Crown and thus 'make merit' to offset a serious cholera epidemic.

Another traumatic event was a great fire which entirely destroyed the Baptist Mission property, including the dwellings, chapel, printing press and stock of books, early in 1851. The newly-printed edition of the New Testament was completely destroyed. The origin of the fire is unknown, but quite possibly it was arson.

After King Mongkut came to the throne in 1851 such antagonism completely disappeared in the capital. However, there was still opposition in the north, and as late as 1869 people were still being put to death. But finally in 1878 the northern missionaries appealed to King Chulalongkorn for freedom of religion, and his Edict of Religious Toleration was the result. A precious document in the history of the Church of Thailand!

In the first sixty years of missionary work, growth had been painful and slow. There were only 600 church members in all — 300 Presbyterians in the south and 150 in the north; 100 Chinese Baptists in Bangkok and 50 Karen Baptists in the north.

A STRONG CHURCH GROWTH MOVEMENT (1884-1914)

At this point one of God's outstanding men appeared on the scene in Thailand — Dr Daniel McGilvary — and an exciting movement towards Christ followed these years of struggles. Both McGilvary and his friend Jonathan Wilson made significant contributions in long lives of missionary service and church planting under the Presbyterian Mission. Both died in the north of Thailand in 1911.

McGilvary and Wilson were men of prayer. Essentially McGilvary's strategy started there, and even as new missionaries they saw the effects of prayer. 'A great respectfulness' in the meetings drew outsiders into the services. Enquirers included students asking for prayer. Wilson wrote, 'Some of them entered into the work with all their might. Their prayers were fervent and their tears flowed for their perishing friends.' This spiritual foundation of prayer supported McGilvary's unshakeable faith, his unbounded vision of the lost and his determination to proclaim Christ, make disciples and establish churches. As a result of the new work he opened in Chiang Mai, the Presbyterians had two distinct missions in Thailand — the Lao (Northern Thai) Mission in the north and the Siam Mission in the south.

In those days the Northern Thai Church began to grow. In 1879 there were fewer than 40 members — five years later there were 152 and the new decade brought the membership to 1841. The awakening movement spread. McGilvary saw the Church grow to over 4,000 before his death in 1911.[1] By 1914 it rose almost to seven thousand, but then the rate of growth was abruptly arrested. The Church plateaued.

Much of the growth in 1892 occurred through famine relief in the Chiang Mai, Lakawn and Prae provinces. In 1904 a corps of medical evangelists travelled about giving vaccinations and spreading the Gospel, as a result of which many converts were won to Christ. Again in 1911 an epidemic of malignant malaria gave increased opportunity for the missionary and national medical evangelists. Frequently in those years a village or family group would send a few representatives to seek out the missionary, to learn of Christ and to request that a teacher be sent to their village. There was a general awakening of interest and a genuine hunger for Christian knowledge across North Thailand. In Chiang Mai at the colony established in 1892 by Dr James McKean for the first systematic treatment of leprosy sufferers, the 700 inmates almost without exception became Christians. The little church at Petchaburi in the south also saw revival and many conversions in the town and surrounding villages, as a few of its members gave themselves to intercessory prayer.

It was during these three decades that the only spectacular growth of the Church in Thailand occurred. From 1914 until recent years it has largely been limited to the children of Christians.

[1] For further information about the life and ministry of Dr McGilvary see section 'How it's done'.

THE PERIOD OF ARRESTED GROWTH (1914-1940)

After 1914 the growth movement was interrupted abruptly. Membership levelled off and between these years the annual growth rate was only 0.7% per annum. Two main causes for this can be identified. First was the lack of shepherding or pastoral care. Those who did believe and were baptized during those years did not continue on. The second reason explains the first — the Presbyterian Mission had changed its policy and strategy. During these years schools and education were emphasized rather than churches and evangelism. Finance was poured into new schools. In 1911 there were 37 mission schools. By 1925 there were 53 and by 1938 there were 65 schools. Priority was given to placing new missionaries in schools. Even more drastically, many missionaries working in churches or in evangelism were withdrawn and transferred to school work. Many ordained Thai church workers were also withdrawn from the churches and placed to teach in the new schools. Thus churches were abandoned, left without leaders. Rural evangelism and extension were stopped.

During those years several new missions arrived in Thailand, including the Seventh Day Adventists and the Christian and Missionary Alliance. In 1934 the Presbyterians reorganized their work, forming a national body called the Church of Christ in Thailand. Other missions later linked with this and it is now the largest Protestant denomination in Thailand.

In 1938-1939 the church was revived through the ministry of the Chinese evangelist John Sung. Particularly among the Chinese churches, nominal Christians were born again, backsliders restored and Christians renewed and purified by God's Holy Spirit. All this helped to prepare the Church for the dark days ahead as it faced the persecution of the war years.

THE CHURCH TESTED DURING THE WAR (1941-1945)

Thailand came under the Japanese during the Second World War and the church suffered. Churches and schools were closed, missionaries interned and pastors forced to seek other employment. Christians who were teachers or local government officials had to repudiate their faith or lose their jobs. Many turned back to Buddhism, putting their income and material security before Christ. Membership of the Church of Christ in Thailand dropped by about one fifth. In spite of this, many who remained true to God had thrilling testimonies of victory in spite of losing their jobs.

POST-WAR RECOVERY AND GROWTH (1946-1978)

At the end of the war a few bold Christian pastors visited the scattered groups of Christians. They taught and encouraged the believers and called the wayward to repentance. Scores confessed and came back to the churches.

The need for evangelism in the post-war period drew many new missionary societies to Thailand: Worldwide Evangelization Crusade and Finnish Free Mission in 1947, Swedish and Norwegian groups in 1949 and Southern Baptists in the same year. Christian Brethren arrived in 1951 as well as the New Tribes Mission. In 1952 the Marburger Mission joined forces with the Church of Christ in Thailand in the northern province of Chiang Rai. The Overseas Missionary Fellowship commenced work in 1952. Between 1960 and 1974 a dozen more new missions came to Thailand, among them several Pentecostal groups and some mass media missions. This period has seen the proliferation of Christian literature in Thailand, the development of other specialist ministries (radio, refugee work, student and Bible college ministries) and extended outreach to tribal groups and Malays.[1]

By 1947 the Church of Christ in Thailand had increased to a membership of 11,756, and by 1970 all Thai churches together had 36,000 members. Today there are some 50,000 adult communicant members.

In 1970 the Spirit of God began to move in many of the village churches in Chiang Rai province in the north of Thailand. Church leaders who had bitter grievances against each other openly confessed their sin and were reconciled to one another. Church members who were gamblers, drunkards or openly immoral were deeply convicted of their sin and broke down with tears. The effect spread to nominal Christians who had not attended church for years, and attendance at services swelled. Witness teams went out to surrounding areas to tell Buddhists that God had become real and meaningful to them.

There were hopes that this movement would spread across the country, but it has remained restricted to only a small area. But its influence has been significant and one result has been a large increase in the number of students attending Bible school.

---

[1] *All mission agencies working in Thailand can be classified under three groups. First are those affiliated with the Church of Christ in Thailand. Second, those who are members of the Evangelical Fellowship of Thailand (EFT), organized in 1970 and recognized by the government. Thirdly, independent groups. The OMF is affiliated with the EFT.*

CONCLUSION (1979- ?)

This seventh period of Thai Church history belongs to us. In December 1978 two days of celebrations were held in the splendid auditorium and grounds of the Bangkok Christian College. The Crown Prince attended the opening ceremony. A combined church choir of over a hundred young Thai people, trained and led by Thai, took part. This, along with exhibits by many churches and Christian groups, was in commemoration of 150 years of Protestant missionary activity in Thailand.

Many Thai churches support their own pastors. Fine young men and women are in training for Christian service. What has been accomplished thrills our hearts and lifts our voices in praise to God. To Him be the glory!

But what are the prospects? The future can be brighter than the past as lessons learned are applied in revised strategy and practice. Opportunities are vast with no laws to restrict the preaching of the Gospel throughout this 'Land of the Free'. Possibilities are exciting.

The present Thai church is a small Gideon's band, a tiny spark of Christian life in the darkness of Buddhism. Many missionary lives have been laid down (21 from the ranks of OMF alone). But with the current favourable spiritual climate, clear vision, bold plans and strong faith, we may well see its greatest increase in our time.

True growth of the Church of the Lord Jesus Christ will only be accomplished by God, through men and women devoted to Him, led of His Spirit in their life and preaching. Let us pray together for this 'Breakthrough'.

QUESTIONS

1. Missionary work usually means facing the difficulties of language, culture and climate. What added difficulties faced the early pioneer missionaries to Thailand?
2. After 150 years of Protestant missionary service in Thailand a mere handful of the population profess faith in the Lord Jesus Christ. Can you suggest three or four reasons why so few have responded?
3. There is a high cost financially and in personnel in establishing institutions such as hospitals and schools. What are the pros and cons of concentrating on these? (You will need to look also at the sections on Central and South Thailand before replying.)

HOW IT'S DONE!

The stories in this section are fictional but based on typical, real-life situations in Thailand.

GROWTH IN THE CITY

During the seven years since Ron had been converted at a University Christian Union meeting he'd had the feeling that God wanted him in overseas missionary work. He subscribed to the magazines of several missionary societies using their prayer calenders regularly. After completing his science degree Ron worked for several years with a petroleum company, led the youth group at his local church and was actively involved in children's missions during the summer holidays. Clearly he needed Bible training, and chose a college which he knew to be missionary orientated.

For practical experience during his second year at college, Ron was appointed assistant pastor at an inner-city church. To his surprise he found there a congregation 90% student and 75% Asian! As the months passed it became evident to Ron and others that the Lord was leading him to a student ministry, and his engagement to Helen was obviously part of it — a former IVCF staffworker, Helen had already been accepted by the same mission to which Ron was applying.

After their arrival in Thailand that inner-city church became their staunchest ally in the struggle to adapt to tropical heat, a strange culture, language, and even, unexpectedly, the unusual habits of fellow-missionaries! Most of those Asian students who'd become their firm friends knew what learning a second language was all about. They could pray with feeling that the distinctions of tone and pronunciation would be heard and reproduced clearly. They prayed for appreciation as well as acceptance of different cultural standards. And they prayed that their friends would love the Thai.

They shared the excitement of a confirmed designation to student work. Ron and Helen would never know the full affect of such prayer support but they never doubted that those who prayed were truly their co-labourers in God's work.

The two long-term goals Ron and Helen set for their first four-year term were: to learn the Thai language well — speaking, reading and writing — and to see Thai young people profess faith in the Lord Jesus Christ.

They asked the Lord for good relationships at the university where Ron lectured as well as in the student-populated area where they lived. They made their home a place where Thai felt relaxed and where they knew they could come and talk about personal needs and problems. English language proved to be an effective tool in evangelism. Apart from ordinary grammar and conversation, English Bible study in small groups proved very popular with young people. They found that, to most university students, religion bears little relevance to daily living. Yet that God-shaped space in the heart of man who is made in the image of God, aches to be filled.

By the end of that four years, nine students had professed faith. Several of these had faced parental opposition; one girl had been beaten and put out of her home by angry parents, and until tempers cooled she had made the missionaries' home her own.

After furlough Ron and Helen found to their

joy that through personal witness there were now twelve believers, even though two of the original nine had turned back and four others had moved to other parts of Thailand.

Several were enquiring about baptism and they were not difficult to prepare for it. One hundred percent literate, with enquiring minds which had already searched out reasons for their faith and made it relevant to life — it was more of a question of confirming basic doctrines through God's Word than of instruction. Eight of the twelve received parental permission and were baptized one Sunday morning by a Thai pastor at his church, some distance away.

For most of the students that church was their nearest, and it took them nearly an hour on a crowded bus to get there. At the next midweek Bible study and prayer meeting at Ron and Helen's home, the students wanted to know why they couldn't begin their own church right there in their own locality. Ron and Helen had been forced to ask themselves the same question and had already prayed about it. Originally they hadn't thought of starting a church. Student work — leading young people to know God and serve Him — had been the sole aim as well as the method of their missionary work. Now, although their methods would not change, they saw a larger goal and wanted to reach for it.

The first practical question, of course, was where to meet. Helen and Ron had borrowed all the books they could lay hold of from fellow missionaries on the subject of church planting principles. They well knew that it was generally not advisable to centre the emerging church in a missionary home, and said so. Nevertheless there was no reasonable alternative since not one student had a home open to use; so after long consideration they decided to use Ron and Helen's sitting room as their 'church', but laid down a time limit of 12 months. In that time (they planned in faith) the group would be larger and able to afford to rent a place.

Sunday Bible Study and worship services were followed by a communal meal and a true family feeling attracted others. Problems and joys were shared together as a group. Answers to their specific prayer requests strengthened faith and the prayer meeting was considered vitally important. Sunday afternoon street witness provided a training ground for these new Christians and through their shaky efforts God blessed and added others. Camping holidays proved very popular. There were losses. As in all student congregations there was a 'floating' element, but overall growth was steadily up.

In their third term of service Ron and Helen wrote to their home church: 'Praise God that the first of our young men has completed Bible training and is now fully supported by the church as their pastor. He and his new wife share our own concern to reach out to other than students in the area of the church. Their rented building is proving almost too small and the Church Committee have launched a Building Fund. Two other young men university graduates are to enter Bible College next month. The most exciting development though is our multiplication by division! Yes, the long-contemplated step was taken three weeks ago. Half the group separated off and now meet in a room loaned to them in another suburb. They are excited by their early contacts and prospects . . . Continue to pray that these young men and women just branching out into careers and jobs will be kept from materialism, kept true to God, and loving in their families where ancestor worship and idolatry are a way of life. May you share our joy and thanksgiving to the Lord Who is building His church.'

> *QUESTION*
> *'Church growth occurs when Christians work hard among a suitably responsive people.' Is this sufficient explanation for Ron and Helen's success? If not, what other factors do you think are relevant?*

WHAT IS A CHURCH?

It's not the building that counts but the people — the 'called out' people of God. The Body of Christ, indwelt by the Holy Spirit, with Christ as its Head and God as its Father. The universal church is that body of believers from every place and of every age. The local church is that group of believers who meet regularly for worship, fellowship and instruction, and to represent the church universal in the local situation.

The Nature of the Local Church

From the very beginning of church planting work the missionary should hold before him the aim of a church being formed, consisting of members who minister to one another and who make their own decisions regarding the work and progress of the group. Encouragement should be given to all to exercise their spiritual gifts and the missionary should explain that, though he may have been used to start the group, he is not their permanent leader. Rather the group should look to God to give gifts of leadership to members within it. Teaching should include the nature, ministry, leadership and responsibilities of local churches, and special attention should be given to the qualifications for Elders listed in I Timothy 3.1-7 and in Titus 1.5-9.

The local Church is

A *worshipping family* of God. Their relationship with Christ their Lord and Saviour binds them into one family, the family of God whom they unitedly worship. Genuine Christians are not to be detached, isolated, or unconnected believers but functionally united as responsible members of His church.

A *sharing fellowship*. Each has the right to approach God directly. Being washed from his sins in the blood of Christ he is made a priest unto God. In addition to this, as 'members one of another', each one has a distinct and responsible relationship to each other. Walking in the light we have 'fellowship with one another'.

A *working community in witness and service*. The Church is God's working representative on earth. Each member is His ambassador. Each is responsible to be in harmony with God and effective in witness and service to the unconverted.

> *QUESTIONS*
> 1. *Can you find Scripture references which show the Church to be a worshipping family, a sharing fellowship and a working community?*
> 2. *The building isn't the most important part of a church — and yet it **is** important. Try to assess the implications for a small group of Christians without anywhere to meet. What advantages would a building give them?*

STARTING FROM SCRATCH

Mike was 32 years old when he arrived on the mission field. It was the culmination of a lifetime of preparation. Godly parents had committed him to the Lord from the day of his birth. He had no memory of any time when God was not awesomely real or when the Lord Jesus was not a loving, present Friend. Mike loved the house of God, and the beautiful stone chapel of his home town was perfection to him with its crimson carpets, stained glass, gleaming brass and the glorious music of its old pipe organ. God's presence was most really to be felt in that sacred place. Following a renewal experience in his teens Mike took a more serious interest in the missionaries who were frequent visitors in his home. It was no surprise to anyone when, on completion of his teaching commitment he entered theological college and took ordination. What did surprise people, himself as much as anyone, was that, following a missionary convention in their town, Mike and Joan his wife made application to an interdenominational missionary society.

Two and a half years later, initial language study completed, Mike and Joan were designated to work in a provincial town in Central Thailand. Missionaries had never been resident there before but, in the overall plan, this growing town was considered a strategic one into which to place two 'church planting couples'. The term amused Mike and Joan. It hadn't been part of their vocabulary until they joined the mission, but they'd been welcomed to fill one of the many listings across the Thailand area for church planters. Life here could hardly be more different from their home town, but they were deeply joyful to be here. The relentless, enervating heat, monotonous flat rice fields, even the separation from their two children away at the mission school in Malaysia — adapting to all this and more, they knew, was part of what it would take of themselves to plant churches.

Mike remembered their first meal in the simple home on high stilts. Trunks of their belongings, yet to be unpacked, lay about them but they were ravenous after the journey up from Bangkok. Mike gave thanks for their packed lunch and began to eat. Suddenly Joan asked him, 'How *do* you plant a church, Mike?'

The question rang in his mind for a long time afterwards. How indeed! Their home country was full of churches. Who'd 'planted' them? Maybe it was only on the mission field that churches had actually to be planted by sheer hard work and agonizing prayer. In the West didn't you just use the ones that were there or, as a group, save up and build a new one? This jolted Mike. How could he, an ordained minister, imply by such thoughts that a church is primarily a building!

Mike had in fact answered Joan directly, 'I don't know, but we've got Dave to learn from.'

Ordained minister though he was, Mike was extremely grateful to God for the man who was to be his senior missionary and co-worker. Dave was American, Brethren by denomination, a year younger than Mike. Yet in their first term in Thailand Dave and his wife Cheryl had seen Thai villagers won to the Lord and formed into a group which was still regularly meeting in another province. Mike suspected that there would be areas in which their different denominational convictions would sometimes collide, but he liked this crew-cut farmer with his southern drawl. Dave and Cheryl had moved up ten days ago and got their own house, two streets away, set up, as well as doing some alterations to this one. Two days later when Mike and Joan were

pretty well organised in their house they joined Dave and Cheryl for their first team meeting.

Joan's question flashed through Mike's mind again as Dave opened the Word of God and bowed in prayer. Then as the farmer read the Scriptures from Matthew 16.13-18 the clergyman and his wife heard as if for the first time the authoritative declaration of the Lord Jesus — 'I will build my Church', Dave went on to answer their question. The builder is the Lord. Their part? — proclaimers. The foundation of the building is a personal confession that Jesus Christ is the Son of the one true, living God. That confession did not result from reasoning alone but was revealed from the Father in Heaven. The triune God was involved in building the Church but He requires the feet, the voice, the strength and heart, and above all the faith, of men and women, to do the job.

They would tramp Thai soil, stammer Thai language, love and work and preach and pray but, miraculously, it would be the Holy Spirit of God who would open blind Thai eyes, cause them to make that great confession of faith, give them new life and make of them His Church. And this would be the burden of the missionaries' praying from the beginning.

HOW DO YOU PLANT A CHURCH?

Central Thailand field policy (within which Mike and Dave were working) gives the following outline:
Phase 1: First contact, cultural adaptation, language learning.
Phase 2: Basic evangelism. Saturation of the area with basic knowledge.
Phase 3: Teaching prospective leaders, involving others in evangelism while continuing in widespread evangelism yourself.
Phase 4: Training leaders. Involving members more and more and the missionary less and less. At this stage no longer living in the town or village concerned.
Phase 5: Withdrawal.

QUESTIONS
1. Could this basic outline apply in our situation here at home? Or how should it be modified?
2. What is your local church doing about planting daughter churches?

Putting it into practice

Mike and Dave debated methods of evangelism. They agreed to aim for leaders of families and family groups. In most cases heads of families were men who were available only in the evenings. It would mean overnight visits to outlying villages, getting to know such men in the setting of their home and family. The dry season, when farmers were free from their heaviest work in the rice fields, would naturally be chosen for this village work, while in the town evangelism could more easily be planned as a year-round programme.

They would set themselves measurable goals so as to be able to assess progress realistically. For instance they could not, in one dry season, thoroughly evangelize all the villages of their area. Lasting commitments to Christ made in faith need also a basis of knowledge. This cannot be assumed to be present as perhaps it can in the West. In this Buddhist/animistic climate, failure to clarify terms and lay a foundation of clear, basic doctrine will lead to syncretism and compromise. So prior to calling for decisions, there had to be a thorough preparation by teaching.

Mike and Dave appreciated too that a basic principle of church growth was through family relationships — Thai witnessing to their extended families so that whole related groups may be brought into the Church.

The essence of simplicity on paper, in practice the strategy took years to accomplish. There had to be a balance between faith and sheer hard work. They well knew that God's grace cannot be reduced to a formula. Missionaries of stronger faith than theirs had not always seen churches established; despite years of work some had seen little response.

Mike and Joan studied and improved their language, adapted to Thai culture, visited homes and welcomed visitors. The two couples set a goal for their prayers, asking friends at home to join them, that two families would believe within 12 months. The two men used literature, used the Word of God, preached in the market, preached in the villages. Months passed and they registered an area of town, a few families, warming to their message. In rural areas ties of kinship remain generally strong, and a community of believers comprising families will less easily fall to opposition than will isolated individuals. The youngest child of one of these families, Mr & Mrs Boon, died, and the sorrowing parents and neighbours read true sympathy in the faces of those four foreigners. They heard compassion in the American's voice as he spoke from the book of his God, and they wondered if it could be true that for those who believed in Jesus there was forgiveness of sins, a Saviour to help, one rebirth now and, after death, eternity with God.

A Thai evangelist visited at the invitation of the missionaries. Over a week of meetings he explained from the Scriptures the answers of God to life and death. The miracle happened. The Holy Spirit gave understanding, repentance and faith. With indescribable joy Mike heard the first confessions of faith in the Lord Jesus Christ and watched the destruction of various charms and idols in which these new believers, from three families, had previously trusted. They had accepted the 'one way' of Jesus. There was no place now for the old accessories of darkness. How carefully the Thai preacher emphasized this, questioning in detail about any such items remaining in the houses of these five new Christians.

QUESTIONS

Now there have been some conversions, the work takes on a new dimension. Many new questions need thinking through and answering.

1. How are these new Christians to be taught? A policy would need to be worked out. Factors to bear in mind:
    Lack of background of Christian teaching
    Certainty they would face testing, temptation and discouragement
    Some will probably be only semi-literate
   Ideas to consider:
    Have a period of instruction before baptism
    Regular visiting by missionary
    Teaching them to use the Bible (should the missionary give them one — or a NT?)
    Correspondence course, Bible study notes, catechism courses, cassettes, teaching through John's gospel.

2. Think again of the first few pages describing life in Thailand and the background of Buddhism. Then draw up a simple outline of basic truths that a new Christian in a Buddhist/Animist environment needs to know. Can you think of two or three subjects he would need teaching about of which we in the West have little experience?

3. One of the believers sells food on the market for a living. Ought the missionaries to insist from the outset that she shouldn't sell on Sundays, or let that come gradually from conviction?

4. Where are meetings to be held?
   — in the missionary's house?
   — in the house of one of the Christians?
   — in a building paid for by the missionary or his friends at home?
   (Will it then be considered a foreign based operation? Will the Christians appreciate the benefits of having a building if they don't have to work for it themselves?)

Can't we help?

Joan was thinking often these days of a particularly poor family in one of the villages who were showing interest. Their children were thin and their few clothes old and shabby. 'Could we help the Wannee family financially?' she asked. 'Wouldn't that be a witness to others of our love and caring in a practical way?'

Cheryl smiled, hearing herself in the question. 'Dave and I learned some unforgettable lessons in our first term', she responded. 'As you know, our work was with villagers and they were the poorest people we'd ever seen. Despite mission regulations we gave them the clothes we thought they needed, and pretty soon they were begging for more. We gave them free medicine and even loans of cash. It wasn't long before we realised that half of our rapidly-growing flock were "rice Christians" pure and simple. It was a lot harder to stop than it had been to start, and we lost about twenty "believers". From that time on we not only introduced church offerings but taught tithing. They were never rich, but the Lord honoured their giving and before we left for furlough we saw them beginning to put together their own simple chapel, which they were providing.

'We never want a repeat of the shame and heartache of those early days. People lose their self-respect when we give unwisely, and putting them in our debt is wrong. Besides, it's vital for them to learn to look to the Lord to supply their needs, not to us.'

The catechisms arrived and the one they chose was used in conjunction with other methods of instruction. Scripture memorization, using texts related to basic truths, was popular from the beginning with adults and children alike. God's Word 'hid in the heart' does its own work. The missionaries rejoiced and marvelled at the rapid growth in understanding and changes in the lives of the Christians. The first strangely formal, hesitant prayers gradually assumed the confidence of those who begin to see answers and learn to trust their Heavenly Father. Prayer grew more important and the witness of their lives and words bore fruit.

QUESTION

To give or loan money in Thailand puts the one helped under the power of the helper. Chinese money lenders use this kind of power to manipulate poor farmers. How can the missionary help the poor in the community without getting into this kind of situation?

WHAT IS GROWTH?

Quantitative (numerical) growth cannot be properly assessed except by careful recording of decisions, those who go on to baptism and who continue in church membership, as well as reversions. A large church of several hundred members may in fact be static growthwise whilst a small group which increases 10—15 members over a year is a growing church. Visualisation of gains and losses is a simple and useful method of recording.

In Acts 14.21-23 we see three aspects of growth, some of which can be measured by man, some of which only God can judge:
v.21 The Church in Derbe had grown *numerically* — 'they taught many.'
v.22 It was growing *spiritually* — confirming, exhorting, continuing in the faith 'through much tribulation'.
v.23 *Organizationally* — ordaining of elders. Beginnings of self-government.

Not by work alone

As expected there were conflicting opinions between Dave and Mike on several issues, but usually they were able to come to an agreeable solution. Despite his denominational bias Mike readily accepted that baptism by immersion was to be the norm. He was tempted to hold out for the use of real bread instead of local substitutes for communion and it was difficult for him to adapt to the use of hymns to local tunes rather than 'good old' western translated ones. Other questions they spent a lot of time over related to church finances — who should hold the money, how should it be administered, when to introduce tithing, 'Poor Fund' etc. How soon to elect officers; forms of discipline; one-man-ministry — questions like these had been black and white for Mike in the security of a structured denomination at home, but now needed to be thought through in a different light. The field policy statement was a sensible and clear-cut outline hammered out in the early years of work in Central Thailand by missionaries of widely differing backgrounds, and they continually made reference to that.

How often they wanted to push! As numbers grew and funds became available the purchase of land and building plans were discussed. Western impatience and drive learned to sit back, hold itself in check, and wait, on this and many other matters.

Mike had never worked harder. Evangelistic trips to outlying villages probing for responsiveness . . . repeat visits to follow up and teach . . . preparation for his own periodic language exams . . . guiding the expanding town group . . . leadership training weekends. Cheryl and Joan added women's and children's meetings to their literacy work and trained young people to teach in the Sunday School.

But hard work and human effort alone will never build a healthy indigenous church. The missionaries taught the new believers that prayer — individual and corporate — was essential, and needed to watch carefully that their own busyness did not stifle spiritual freshness. They themselves had surrounded the Christians by their prayers and from the beginning urged their prayer companions at home to do the same.

By God's grace they saw the town church planted and growing and little groups of villagers believing. Packing for furlough, Joan remembered her question to Mike that first day, 'How do you plant a church?' She was glad that they did not have any pat answer even now. Certain procedures were advisable, faith and self-expenditure were essential, but 'the builder is God'.

QUESTIONS
1. 'Church Planters' are generally in shorter supply than are 'specialist missionaries.' Why is this? What qualities do you think are essential for a church planter?
2. What advantages and disadvantages will the trained minister or clergyman have as compared with a layman church planter? (e.g. Mike and Dave). How valuable is home church experience before the missionary goes abroad as a church planter?

GROWTH IN THE PAST

Why did the Church in Thailand experience such rapid growth during the ten years after 1884, when church membership in the North increased from 152 to 1841? What spiritual dynamics were at work. What strategy was applied that may be lacking today?

God's methods are men (Acts 1.8) and one of the men most used of God in Thailand was Dr Daniel McGilvary.[1] Daniel McGilvary received Christ following the evangelistic ministry of a Methodist named Brainerd and also came under the influence of campus revivals at Princeton USA in the 1850's. A study of the life and letters of Daniel McGilvary reveals some of the reasons why God blessed his church planting ministry.

A. McGilvary believed that church growth was intensely spiritual. It was the divine activity of God. Therefore:
Christ's Gospel must be preached in its fulness as the power of God unto salvation. God's holiness and power are to be emphasized as well as His love. The Word of God must be taught and obeyed to see genuine fruit in lives.

B. McGilvary himself was a deeply spiritual man. He exhibited the spiritual qualities required for spiritual warfare (Ephesians 6). He was a man of *prayer*. Victory came as he bound the strong man through intercession. He called the churches to regular seasons of prayer. He believed in the *power of the Holy Spirit*. He had experienced the power of God in the evangelical awakenings in the USA and through his student days on campus. He took that dynamic of the Spirit with him in his work.

He was a man of *faith*. He had unshakeable confidence in the sovereign Lord over all. He compared the task in Thailand against great odds to Joshua taking the promised land. He was willing to sacrifice and suffer persecution and difficulties, determined to obey God above all else. He had a pioneering spirit, a deep love for the Lord Jesus Christ and a burden to win the lost for Him. He had clear goals and set out to make disciples and plant the church. He wrote, 'A Christian Church and a Christian constituency must be the first aim in all missions.'

He identified with the people, empathized with their local problems, lived, slept and ate with them in order to share Christ. He loved the people. There is no substitute for these qualities in today's church planter.

God has revealed certain principles in His Word for evangelism and church growth.[1] McGilvary followed these.

1. God is interested in quantity. He wants us to sow the Gospel seed widely. McGilvary was often away from home for three to four months at a time reaching remote areas, even up till he was 80 years of age. He introduced new missionaries to this itinerating also.

2. God is interested in quality as well as quantity. So was McGilvary. Like Paul he travelled widely visiting the young churches and converts. He nurtured, taught and counselled them. He was concerned to educate the illiterate so they

[1]*For a more detailed discussion of what has come to be called 'Church Growth Methods' the reader is referred to* Strategy for Multiplying Rural Churches in Thailand *by Alex. G. Smith,* How Churches Grow *and* Bridges of God *by D.A. McGavran, and many other similar titles.*

could read the Scriptures and grow. He encouraged them to use their spiritual gifts in witness and service to the community and in ministries within the Church.

3. Since he did not remain long with any one group local churches did not become dependent on him. McGilvary committed the young churches to the Holy Spirit, believing God to keep them as they prayed, read the Word of God and worshipped together.

4. He encouraged them to be financially self-supporting.

5. In his travelling he sought to identify responsive individuals, families and groups. God's Word teaches us to major on responsive areas.

6. He emphasized disciple-making and brought these disciples together in community. He always aimed to plant churches, even among a few believing families out in the woods.

7. McGilvary planned for church growth. He had a wide vision, not only for Thai but tribal groups as well. He sent his best workers and associates to pioneer new areas. He taught new groups to reach their own friends and neighbours. In this way whole families, extended families and villages came to Christ.

8. McGilvary sought responsible older men to be leaders. His method of training them was of the apprentice type, taking the best men with him on tours and visits so that they would learn from his example. He studied the Word with them. Later he introduced concentrated training sessions of several weeks for leaders of various areas. Mature leadership was vital in the rapidly-growing Church.

May God help us to follow these principles.

SOMETHING TO THINK ABOUT

1. [1]Is evangelism an end in itself? What is its purpose and goal? (See Matthew 28.18-20) What do the terms 'proclamation' and 'persuasion' mean in the context of evangelism?

2. How do you think a missionary should work to plant churches that are:
a) self-supporting — in the area of finances, b) self governing — in the area of leadership, c) self propagating — in the area of outreach?

[1] See also section 'The First 150 Years'.

CENTRAL THAILAND

THE FIRST FIVE YEARS

Enthusiastic young Australian Leon Gold spoke up, 'There are 150 CIM/OMF missionaries in Thailand because China closed. This is God's hour for Thailand!'

The others at the 1953 annual missionary conference agreed, gripped by the optimism, the urgency. Thailand for Christ now, before it suffered China's fate! But twenty years later Leon Gold died of cancer and neither the Communists nor God's hour had come.

The last missionaries of the China Inland Mission were still straggling out of China in 1951 as the first missionary of the CIM Overseas Missionary Fellowship, Miss Beugler, arrived in Bangkok. American Presbyterian missionaries had worked long and hard for over a hundred years to establish churches in Bangkok and Chiang Mai. But the thirteen provinces of Central Thailand were virtually untouched. The nearest a missionary had ever come to Manorom where now a church and hospital stand was when she died during a river journey between Chiang Mai and Bangkok and had to be buried there. Amazingly, Central Thailand had been by-passed by the Christian world. It was still a pioneer area, yes; but not primitive. An eager new worker, Grace Harris, set out by train for the first upcountry base. SARABURI. That's what her Superintendent had written on the card. Consternation an hour later when she saw that there were no English signposts!

Suddenly, a Thai gentleman leant over and asked in English if he could help. He explained that Saraburi did not even adjoin the railway! Their conversation was exceptional for almost no English was understood in the central provinces, but Grace never forgot that many of the Thai in this unreached land were well-educated and travelled. And yet . . . hardly any of the three million mostly farming people in these 24,000 square miles of paddy field and picturesque rocky wooded hill had ever heard of the Name of Jesus. Two tiny churches existed to cater for two tiny pockets of Chinese residents who worshipped in a Chinese dialect; and that was all.

By January 1953 a couple of missionaries were resident in each of eight provincial capitals. They rented unprepossessing unpainted wooden houses on stilts. One home was in a riceyard and visitors had to squeeze up through a trap-door; another was flanked by pigsties and rubbish dumps. What was important was that the new-comers were living inconspicuously at the level of any other teacher. It didn't take long for them to discover that the Chinese they had painfully learnt in China was almost useless here.

The Chinese in the markets were learning Thai too; and the prevailing dialect was one none of them had ever learnt anyway. For the sake of speed, the first books and tracts were translated from Chinese or English by a Thai who spoke Chinese, printed in Hong Kong at the Christian Witness Press, and sold in little packs costing one baht. Many new missionaries became extremely fluent in their one and only pat Thai sentence, 'Chut le baht!' Others rose early, boiled up a pot of glue, then proceeded to paste up Thai Scripture posters on the obligingly-located trees flanking the roads and rivers. Hand-wound record players with a Thai track guaranteed a fascinated

crowd. Hordes of inquisitive children gazed at every movement of the big-nosed foreigners, peeking through the ill-fitting wall and floor-boards, or listening appreciatively to the first faltering Bible stories in Thai. Everyone was friendly and many most anxious to learn English. Not a few missionaries, struggling with the tonal language, found the teaching of English Bible a welcome relief!

During the first year a survey party was sent through the region in order to plan a strategy suited to Central Thailand. Mission leaders Mr Butler and Dr Broomhall were accompanied by the intrepid interpreter Emerson Frey, who qualified for the job because he had been there for a whole six weeks! The observations of the survey party were reported back to the team: Central Thailand had a vast network of heavily-populated waterways and only a few fine-weather roads. Chainat province was the natural centre for waterway communications. There was a definite medical need in the predominently rural areas. 'We could without difficulty apply all our medical forces in this country.' They recommended a medico-evangelistic launch and later a small hospital in Chainat province. The high incidence of leprosy was noted along with the lack of any care, due to the fact that leprosy was regarded as the result of the sufferer's sin.

The new evangelistic launch was soon providing an extremely cramped home for the first two sailors, Em Frey and Isaac Scot. Once the latter, a six-foot ex-policeman, had crawled into position at the rear he could no longer see navigator Em who (with no previous experience steering a boat) shouted intriguing directions. As a result, the first missionary journey took them straight across the river into the side of a rice barge. While Isaac blushed, Em offered the irate owner a disarming smile and a tract. A smile in the Land of Smiles was always an acceptable escape mechanism. Peter Draper had similar navigational difficulties when the boat approached a plank bridge lined with laughing laundry ladies. Within seconds the boat had nudged both bridge and beauties into the water. Undaunted, the chivalrous foreigner waited till they surfaced and offered them Christian literature. And so 17,475 Scripture portions were sold in the first year of operation. Eventually a larger, more suitable vessel named SANTISUK or Peace Launch, was built and used extensively along the waterways.

Following the recommendations of the survey, missionary doctors and nurses arrived in Bangkok and, after passing the Thai government medical exams, were licensed to practise in Thailand. A Thai government spokesman indicated that OMF medical expertise could best serve Thailand through quality care in hospitals, while the government would endeavour to develop basic public health services. Two small clinics were opened in market towns in 1954. Wiset, meaning 'Special Place', was basically three dirty markets with an opium den in the centre. How the team prayed that it would become a special place for many as they found complete healing in Christ. Inburi clinic was supposed to start quietly as an experiment but the doctor was soon submerged under nearly six hundred registrations. At both of these and other centres the first patients started receiving medicine for leprosy. By 1956 Drs Chris and Catherine Maddox had gone on to see Manorom Hospital established in a low-lying paddy-rice basin in Chainat province; later still a residential clinic was opened in the remote Nongbua market in the north-east of the region. Law, order, and medical care were lacking here due to the district's being far from the river and road network. The long rainy

season turned the buffalo cart tracks into seas of mud which repelled any vehicle more modern than the elephant.

By 1954 the missionaries' willingness to take every opportunity to make Christ known in spite of inadequate language paid off, and the first few believers were baptized at Paknampho, known formally as Nakhon Sawan city. The Superintendent wrote jubilantly to his team: 'Perhaps *this* is the breaking forth of blessing!' The first believers were very conscious of their isolation and baptismal days became opportunities for Christians to gather from all over Central Thailand, bringing their food with them. They were encouraged to evolve their own structure and church organization and what developed was a congregational pattern with lay leadership, and authority vested in the annual believers' conference. At this a committee was elected to manage affairs and maintain communication between the various groups. The occasional group functions met a great need, for most festivals were Buddhist and community based, the only outlet for fun; and fun was a virtue in Thailand.

'When you are talking to me, I feel I can believe, but when I go home . . .' the housegirl in Wiset didn't need to finish her sentence. Her dilemma was typical. Being interested and professing to believe was one thing, but to be baptized publicly and follow Christ only was like social suicide in a society that prized conformity above right or wrong. To be a Thai was to be a Buddhist. How could life continue to be pleasant if one was anything else? And to trust Christ's power rather than placate evil spirits — was trust enough? Initial crowds and bright interest faded as what it really meant to become a Christian dawned on visitors to the missionaries' homes. Occasionally teenagers were forbidden to continue contact. Children, it seemed, were a law unto themselves. After five years it became apparent that the clarion call, 'Now is God's hour for Thailand!' had not been fulfilled in a manner the missionaries could see and rejoice in. Where was the rich harvest? How much longer must they plough and sow and wait?

Thousands of friendly Thai had heard the message but few responded personally. Modern language techniques were still in the future and the early missionaries struggled to make the Gospel intelligible in spite of recurr-

ing mistakes. One consonant change and 'the Cross' turned into 'a pair of trousers' during one earnest sermon. Many were dogged by one illness after another. Dengue fever stole years of missionary time with its severe joint pains, headaches, persistant fevers and resultant depression. The few Thai who became Christians had yet to appreciate the value of regular meeting together on Sundays or for prayer. All services had to be held in missionary homes although the aim was to find somewhere neutral as quickly as possible. But misunderstandings arose and the meetings foundered if they were moved prematurely into Thai homes in those early years.

1955 was a year of depression for the missionary team. But in retrospect they were reassured that God had been quietly at work, for in that year two of the key men in the growth of the Church in Thailand were converted.

Mr Arphon was a well-educated man who had studied Buddhism deeply and thoroughly. His interest in Christianity began when he attended English Bible classes run by missionaries at Paknampho, and ultimately he accepted the irresistible claims of the Jesus about whom he was learning. This diminutive, diplomatic bachelor soon became a giant in the faith. He served Manorom Hospital as a faithful business manager for many years before going to Laos to work with Asian Christian Service in a medical programme. Today he is the General Secretary of the Evangelical Fellowship of Thailand, and his unobtrusive, untiring, wise and spiritual ministry has contributed much to the Church; as has his example in resisting the desire for material gain. His personality has encouraged and challenged the missionary team.

The first link in the chain to lead Mr Samyong to Christ was his love for children. Two missionary's toddlers were playing up on the verandah of their home, and shy smiles were exchanged between the young man in the street and the children up above him. Samyong, an actor, began to visit the children and was quickly accepted and loved in the home. He slowly began to welcome the message of truth about the living God which their father shared with him. The second link was his love for music, as he found these Christian missionaries singing about a Saviour, and the third was the deep effect that the words he read in a Christian tract had upon him — a tract he received when standing half hidden in the crowd at a children's meeting.

Samyong was used to the life of an actor, and found that life as a Christian conflicted with much of his former life-style. He left the troupe and blossomed as a steady Christian with marked musical, preaching and teaching gifts. The first hymn books were translated from Chinese or English, and the Thai words had to be crammed or stretched to fit the foreign tunes which were hard for many country Thai to remember. Samyong has given the church scores of beautiful indigenous hymns, some set to traditional tunes and all with deep spiritual meaning. And he enriches Christian gatherings by playing the curved wooden xylophone, or by his singing. He was always eager to join evangelistic teams, and because of his ability as a Bible teacher he spent several years at Phayao Bible Training Centre before his work at the 'Voice of Peace' radio studio in Chaing Mai. Today he is chairman of the Thai Home Missions Board, and is working on gathering up other talented converted actors in order to establish a Christian musical acting troupe to use in evangelism.

The conversion of these two men encouraged the missionary team to go on in faith, believing God's promises that fruit would result.

TO HELP THE MAIMED

Tall and slim, Dr Catherine Maddox stood before the annual missionary conference to give the first report on leprosy work. It was a moving one. Two men had accepted the medicine offered in return for a small sum weekly. Many others watched to see what would happen. The strange white nurses dared to touch the repulsive feet and cut away the dead flesh from the leprosy sufferers! Why were these women so ready to humble themselves and touch the outcast? Was it merit-making to offset some great sin, or did they really care because their God did? Within a year one hundred patients had joined those first two in one centre alone; they began to receive, not only weekly treatment, but also a wonderful new message of love and hope. The response was quick and real. Who better than a leprosy sufferer could understand that in heaven he would have a glorious, perfect, heavenly body? As Dr June Morgan, the present leprosy doctor, likes to say, 'My lame leprosy patients will be among those who leap for joy!' Some were baptized that first year.

But there was a problem, and Dr Catherine voiced it.

'What is to be the place in the young Church of the patients who have believed? The Thai ostracise those with leprosy—and sound public health teaching means they should be kept separate. Yet must prejudice be encour-

aged at the expense of human love? Must we encourage two parallel churches when there is barely a handful of believers in any one place?'

An energetic discussion broke out with considerable difference of opinion. A medical worker made her point bluntly.

'It's no good teaching public health and not showing it in practice during a Sunday meeting.'

'That's right,' said another nurse, 'and we can encourage well and leprosy believers to show mutual love and interest in each other in prayer and less obvious ways.' But even medical opinion was sharply divided.

'That's all very well, but let's face it, segregation hinders rehabilitation and it's not good for the patient either socially or spiritually. We are trying to keep the social problems from escalating; and we should do the same in the church.'

Em Frey seemed to be thinking aloud as he spoke, 'At the moment, the Sunday services are in our missionary homes; and as we don't mind, both well and leprosy believers can come. But eventually the decision must rest with the Thai churches. What will in fact happen when they get their own places of worship?'

Dr Catherine looked at her watch. 'I suggest we stop for lunch,' she said.

Em and Grace Frey returned to their little palace among the pig pens in the historic city of Lopburi. There was a letter waiting from son Ricky, away at school; and a bundle of tracts Em had designed and had printed. Lopburi Christian group was developing in a manner typical of the other centres. At least half were medical contacts and the number of severely-deformed leprosy believers was growing. At the same time, higher class people were turning to Christ, like Mrs Jit who helped with writing informative letters between the churches, as well as other literature and language work, and who later prepared material for the Thailand Bible Society. The missionaries encouraged the Christians in the vision of their own place of worship. One Christian donated a clock for the as-yet non-existent building, but by 1956 there was a small sum in the bank towards it. Again the missionaries tried not to influence the believers in marking out a line between 'leprosy' and 'well'. Lacking suitable land for a building, the well believers rented a house near the railway station for a time, used the missionary's home, and then met in a school. The leprosy believers started to meet in the treatment place, a wooden shelter (or 'sala')[1] on the parapets of the ancient city wall. That simple sala meant so much to them. From being failures in their society, they had there become acceptable and victorious soldiers of Jesus Christ. Loneliness could be forgotten when they met for fellowship together.

Miss Gong's disease and disfigurements meant she could not go out to work. She stayed home to mind children and her father. She resigned herself to never having any friends, and to never getting out. One day a family member brought news of the leprosy treatment sala, and timidly she went along. Miss Ubon, a bright leprosy Christian, sat beside her and asked, 'Where do you live?'

They chatted. Relief! She was accepted in this place. Each time she went to the sala Miss Ubon was waiting to greet her, and as they talked, the Christian gave her testimony of all that Jesus had done for her. Miss Gong wondered, 'Why does she befriend me?' One day Miss Ubon said, 'I'll meet you here at church on Sunday.' It was just a casual invitation. She felt so nervous yet so eager to go. And on arrival she found everyone just as

[1] *Sala*—Thai word meaning any small wall-less public shelter from rain and sun.

genuinely friendly as Miss Ubon. Mr Hit in particular was very conscious of her presence. 'What a pity she isn't a Christian', he thought. She matched his ideal for a wife. He was a builder by trade, with face and hands badly scarred by leprosy. But he was developing a deep love for God and His Word through the excellent regular Bible teaching at the sala. Reading the Bible was slow and laborious for him and he had to think long and hard over its practical application to everyday life. That's where the presence of the others was so invaluable. They could talk problems over as they arose. A spell at the Manorom Hospital leprosy wing was a spiritual booster too. People walking past that wing would frequently hear bursts of laughter, animated discussion in a spontaneous Bible study, vigorous hymn singing to the accompaniment of traditional Thai instruments; and near Christmas see the play practices in the old theatrical style. There was the serious one-to-one talk with staff members or fellow patients as they learned trades in the rehabilitation block. With help like this, Mr Hit was able to stick to his decision not to marry a non-Christian, a pitfall many 'well' Christians fell into. He prayed for Miss Gong's conversion; and as soon as God had answered his prayer, wasted no time in collecting a senior relative and heading unannounced for Miss Gong's home! Today they have a happy Christian home and Mr Hit has built another sala in a more distant spot so that the nurses can treat even more patients with physical and spiritual medicine.

With prolonged nurture of this kind over a decade or more, it was little wonder that most of the mature Christians were those with leprosy. It was rich reward for the hard-working leprosy nurses. Although they were helped by a church-planting missionary, it was these ladies, only two or three to a centre, who bore the brunt of the work. By 1978 they were caring for 3,000 patients. The team in Lopburi had to cover four provinces through clinics and home visits, and were only too familiar with long, weary journeys on motorbikes through thick dust or thick mud. For them everyday life might include a tumble where a little bridge was faulty; the occasional hold-up in a lonely spot; vicious dog bites during a home visit; counselling a whole family on marital problems, pig disease, monetary loans or the latest theft; literacy lessons; minor cassettophone repair; slow deliberate teaching of Bible truth to a mind dulled by minimal education, vitamin deficiency, and fear of evil spirits. It was all Christ-like service that God honoured.

The maturity of the leprosy Christians showed itself in their more vigorous 'sala' churches committee and annual conference which both parallelled the 'well' church structure. The sala believers met annually at Uthaithani, where there was the first church building in Central Thailand. Christian G.I.s had once helped improve the facilities, and the serial numbers on old ammunition boxes which made up the wall behind the preacher's head were a moving reminder that here the battle was the Lord's, that He had brought peace to Thai hearts. Because the lines between leprosy and well were never defined, and because many well relatives of patients had believed through the clinics and through seeing the change in hopeless lives, many rural well believers preferred to attend the more populous 'sala' conference of up to two hundred — the other might have only twenty or so living in at a rented school!

Gradually, with improved modern medicines, leprosy ceased to be the fearsome disease of former years; many were pronounced clear and gradually members of one committee began to be represented on the

other. One year five of the eight elected members on the Central Churches Commitee (well) were ex-leprosy patients! In Lopburi the well and sala groups would combine for monthly fellowship meetings. Early in 1975 they discussed the buying of land for a church building. A timely donation for the project from Bangkok Christians did not stipulate whether it was for 'well' or 'sala', and the sala group expressed its desire to join forces in the future with the well believers, helping with finance. Mr Brayat, their most prominent leader, drew up plans for a church. Protracted discussions resulted at national Christian and missionary level. What about the deformed, burnt-out leprosy cases? Wouldn't they put off townspeople still wary of social stigmas like leprosy? Wasn't the move premature? Wasn't it wonderful? The believers looked at Scripture, in Ephesians where it spoke of Christ breaking down barriers between one type of man and another, and made their decision. The missionary team was divided but stood quietly back.

On Chistmas Day, 1976, invitations were issued to all Central Thailand believers to attend the opening of the Lopburi church building. The Manorom Leprosy Wing band provided the musical support; both leprosy and well Christians took leading parts. The government official pulling back the pink gauze from the plaque noted favourably the presence of leprosy and well. He had travelled overseas, he said, and had seen how those who call themselves Christians were able to put aside social barriers in order to be one in Christ.

The bold step of the Lopburi Christians set the ball rolling. The annual conferences both voted to merge and the twenty-five years of parallel church organization came to an end in the year of jubilee. All one in Christ Jesus!

Where does the hospital fit in?

The shrill ringing of the office phone cut through the quiet murmur of voices. Two lady missionaries and a Thai evangelist were praying for the many patients spoken to about Christ. Manorom had quickly grown into a modern, one-hundred-bed hospital and Nongbua clinic was replaced in 1968 by a twenty-five-bed hospital. The evangelists in both places were fully extended. Jean Anderson rolled her wheel chair over to the phone. Before she was crippled by polio she'd been in the medical team. Now she could be fulltime in evangelism! The nurse-aide said Dr John Townsend would like an evangelist to visit Mr Jun in Room 7. 'It'll have to be me,' thought Jean to herself, 'Suraphon's got a whole string of patients to see and a home visit too.'

Jean glanced at the sick man's chart. 'Inoperable cancer, will probably only live a few weeks.' Jean had two simultaneous thoughts. 'Praise the Lord Mr Jun has a chance

to believe before he dies!' and ... 'however does leading terminally ill patents to Christ significantly contribute to the OMF goal of planting churches in Central Thailand?' There was the possibility that relatives might be interested but so much depended on speedy follow-up. Jean chafed with frustration over the continuing difficulties in seeing an effective follow-up system established.

Everything depended on quick contact after a patient left hospital; but the evangelistic staff were too few in number to be able to do this themselves as routine. Medical staff had been granted a non-medical working day so that they could visit interested ex-patients, but in practice that only catered for the needs of a few. Cards were posted out to local missionaries and churches, but usually they could not abandon a busy schedule at once and follow the trail along paddy dykes to an isolated spot unrelated to any developing group of believers — even if the address proffered by the patient was clear. Jean sighed. So often it wasn't.

Mr Jun was thin, emaciated and yellow. Jean recognized him at once — he'd had surgery at Manorom a couple of months previously. He knew her too and remembered what he had heard about the Saviour. Yes, he knew what was wrong with him, with no hope physically. Jean talked to him about heaven and Mr Jun told her how impressed he was by the doctor's desire he should go there. His wife joined in the conversation. They both wanted to know about the resurrection of the body and the reality of heaven.

Jean had noticed that Mr Jun was to return home the next day. Would this be the last

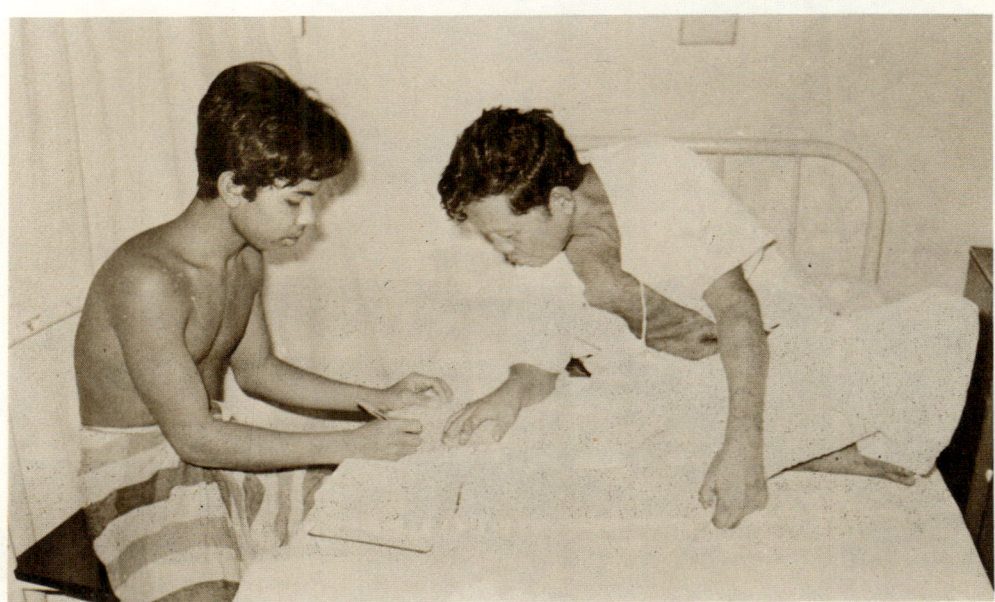

opportunity? She felt compelled to ask him if he was ready to confess his sins and accept Christ as his Saviour. 'Before you do you must take off your spirit string.'

Mr Jun nodded to his wife. She cut off the dirty cord from his neck—it was to keep his spirit from leaving his body. He prayed a simple prayer. That night Thai evangelist Suraphon called in and found a man at peace, rejoicing in anticipation of heaven. The card bearing his name and address was posted off that day. Jean saw to that. Two weeks later the local missionary visited his home. Too late... he'd died. The family were grateful but showed no real interest in the Christian message.

As Jean passed the Isolation Ward she saw through a screen a deathly-white pinched face, an oxygen mask, a blood transfusion bottle. She hesitated before going in. Mr Chalerm had advanced TB and another haemorrhage like the one of a few hours ago would almost certainly be fatal. Would he be able to listen to the Gospel if she made it very simple and repeated it several times?

'Jesus loves you. He is alive and can hear you. He wants to cleanse your heart and make you his child so you can be with him in heaven.' He nodded but was unable to speak. Through subsequent days he rallied a little and soon was enjoying listening to cassettes of Samyong's music. It gripped him as he too had once been in a troupe of actors. Rough country relatives called in and listened too. A church-planting missionary, Rosemarie Hauser, was in close contact with the wife throughout, working in close liaison with Jean. Mr Chalerm died a Christian and Jean put 'finis' to that contact.

But the case hadn't closed. One of the visiting relatives was Mr Boon, a notorious character from Kaw Liaw north of Paknampho. He'd been in Bangkok establishing an alibi as he was planning to kill three men. On his return he heard about his fatally-ill nephew and hurried to see him for the last time. He stayed at Manorom four days, and for the first time heard about Christ through his nephew's testimony, posters, literature, tapes, the intercom radio service and Jean's teaching. Mr Boon wanted to find out more. The next Sunday he went to the Paknampho church, drunk as usual. Two Christian men welcomed him warmly, gave him a Bible and noted his address, called on him regularly till he received Christ and finally saw him baptized by Samyong in July, 1973. His burden for the salvation of others in his district was so infectious that Geoff and Denise Case moved out there for a year before their furlough to work with him. By the time they left there were ten baptized believers in Boon's area, of whom six were his relatives and four were neighbours and friends.

It cheered Jean to find out how God had used hospital evangelism in the building up of His Church. She shared the news with Rosa Brand, another evangelist. Rosa smiled. 'That reminds me of what happened across the river from Mr. Boon's a couple of years ago,' she said.

Already in labour, a young wife was helped into outpatients after a long trip from a remote village where a 'midwife's' insanitary methods and incantations had cost them the life of their firstborn. The lone Christian in their village, a leprosy sufferer, had told them that Manorom Christian Hospital knew how to save little babies. She had given them Christian literature too but it was only as Rosa explained the Gospel that they understood. Mr Kharn, now

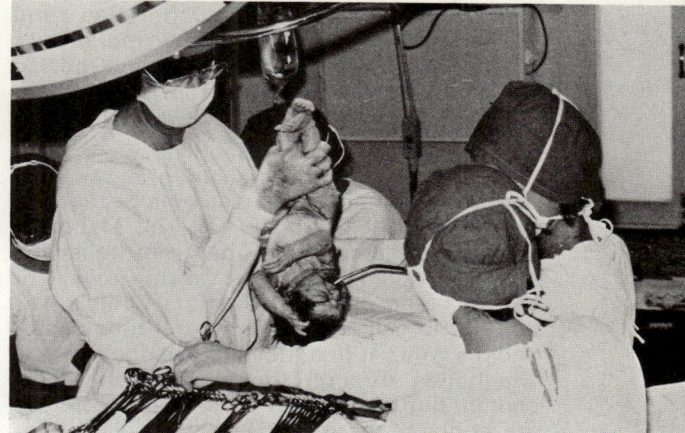

the happy father of a healthy infant, prayed to be born anew. The young mother hesitated. 'I need time to think; and my mother must hear too. Please would you send someone to teach us?' 'Gladly', answered Rosa.

The Paknampho church received the card and set out immediately. Three times they tried but the directions were too poor. So were the roads. They gave up. Two years later the couple reappeared at the hospital for the birth of another child. They spotted Rosa. 'Why haven't you visited us yet?' Rosa felt both the elation and frustration that Jean had. How many contacts were lost this way? This time Rosa took no chances. She arrived at Alan Bennett's door while he was still unpacking from furlough. They tried going by boat and found Kharn. The Paknampho church made monthly visits, feeling the excitement of outreach. By the height of the hot season three months later, twenty were showing interest and five had believed. The Land Rover film team and Phayao Bible Training Centre students moved in for an intensive campaign. In June five were baptized and in July five

more believed. The little church at Ban Yang Yai had a thrilling beginning, set in motion by a leprosy Christian's witness to a loving God and His caring servants at Manorom Hospital.

Right from the start any doubts as to the spiritual efficacy of the medical work were dispelled as one missionary after another reported finding a warm welcome because of the ministry of the hospitals. The Manorom Church itself had twenty baptized believers, mostly hospital employees, within a year or two of being opened. Nongbua Church was the first to call and support a full-time pastor and his wife. At first, hospital evangelism was channelled through the work of the local church, but this did not prove feasible unless the contacts were from the immediate geographical area.

As the years went by the people from nearby villages increasingly appreciated the medical benefits, both curative and preventive care; but increasingly shut their ears to the Gospel. Earnest prayer was offered about this problem and practical steps were taken. In 1974 the church and hospital organised more efficient follow-up with an enlarged team. Dr Ulrich and Adele Juzi and their little boys started to concentrate at weekends on one particular village. They invited the head of the shoe department at the hospital and his wife to join them as a team. The side-benefits of such a plan were obvious and real. Other hospital staff majored on different villages. Rowland Bell visited extensively through the district, determined to explore every slightest interest. His scholarly manner made him highly respected. But still there was only meagre response.

Flood waters rose steadily in October, 1975, and it was soon obvious that the Manorom Basin was in for another disastrous flood with half a million acres of paddy rice destroyed. But this time the hospital staff organized a three-week round-the-clock emergency building up of the dyke-road which runs eight and a half miles along the river by Manorom. Farmers and village folk turned out to help. There had never been such a display of community effort before. The rice crop, market and hospital were saved. And the Christians found that at last there was an openness to the Gospel that had not been there before. 2,500 booklets of the Sermon on the Mount were distributed with both church and hospital addresses on the back. Tiny groups of believers started to meet in the villages on a regular basis, though still very dependent on outside leadership.

One evening in September 1976, Kathie Bell waited in vain for Rowland to return. Then came a message from the hospital. He had been savagely attacked, hit repeatedly in the face with a log by thugs who then stole his bike. In a recent wave of lawlessness others had been held at knife or gun-point before being relieved of their motorbikes; but not previously with bodily injury. Shock rippled through the community that a teacher of Rowland's calibre should be so abused. The abbot of the local temple, already friendly with Rowland, hurried in to express his regret. For weeks Rowland's jellied face had to be supported by intricate scaffolding but the result, his friends said, was better than the original! Rowland continued his visiting, believing that blessing would come.

1978 was the 150th anniversary of Protestant work in Thailand and the 25th jubilee year for OMF in Central Thailand. It was earmarked for evangelism and worldwide prayer for breakthrough. For many Christians around the world, their only concept of Central Thailand was the medical programme. And understandably. Over half the 850 baptized

Christians in the Central provinces were converted through the medical ministry of OMF, either themselves or their relatives having attended the two hospitals or 26 leprosy clinics. Over half the missionary team was engaged in the medical work.

And so when Manorom received international attention on 14th January, 1978 through the tragic road accident that took the lives of five adult missionaries and seven children, including the complete families of two surgeons, the Lord laid it on the hearts of Christians everywhere to pray for Central Thailand as never before. For the missionary team, the shattering repercussions served to deepen hope, expectancy, and increased determination to make Christ known regardless of the cost. Once again shock broke through the impassive resistance in the district and the Lord started to work in hearts previously impervious to the now familiar message. Yet the year 1978 still did not see increased numbers coming into the church, though it did see Christians drawing together in combined efforts in an unprecedented way. A year later at Manorom Hospital, over twenty staff turned to God for the first time or with renewed fervour.

But on the whole, the years of sowing continue, sometimes with tears but always believing that there will be a reaping with shouts of joy. In the interim between sowing and reaping, the team endeavour to wait without discouragement or despair, supported by the prayer of God's people world-wide.

TRAINING THE LEADERS TO LEAD

Dalukdu. A scruffy little village lined with rough coffee stalls catering for thirsty travellers. The travellers were always coming through the hot season's red dust or the rainy season's squelchy mud to visit the shrines in the limestone caves behind the houses. But one hot night in 1960 some new visitors called. A Land Rover bounced over concrete-like ruts, baked by the sun for five rainless months, and some foreigners showed film-strips of an enormous flood that covered the earth. A man called Noah was saved because he believed in God and obeyed Him. For the next two years young Mr Boon Mee pondered the meaning of the strange story. He also pondered his own plight. He had leprosy. Then in March, 1962, he heard of more strange visitors, foreign leprosy nurses, riding push bikes many kilometres from Uthai town, to give unheard-of medical care to leprosy victims. He went to the treatment sala. It was easy to find there on the buffalo cart track leading to the Taptan temple. Fancy these women caring enough to touch maimed limbs! He didn't like the preaching of the foreign man but agreed to start a correspondence course. In May, after one of the 'preaches' he disliked, Boon Mee was led to the Lord by Jim Tootill. Jim quickly led him on to witnessing, preaching at the sala and regular Bible study. Small short-term Bible schools were also arranged for Boon Mee and other young Christians.

Boon Mee was too fresh from Buddhism to forget that suffering and misfortune were regarded as sinful. So he was very vulnerable and uneasy when Satan started to taunt and tempt. He became very ill. Should he turn back from following Christ? Should he seek help in Bangkok? A wonderfully timed home visit by

Ruth Adams resulted in his going to Manorom Hospital. He hadn't dared to think that leprosy patients were welcome there! On his return he found that his young wife had left him. But Boon Mee did not falter. He went instead to North-East Thailand where the Christian and Missionary Alliance had a leprosy Bible school near Khonkaen. Over the four years he became head student and also met Chusee who became his wife. Back home he made himself available for Christian service, preaching in four clinics a month and being elected to the sala churches committee that planned the annual conference and cared for the welfare of the sala believers. He began to show leadership initiative.

'Would the Land Rover film team please come back to Dalukdu area where I live? I'll join the team with you.' As the team visited in the homes they realised how effective Boon Mee's testimony was. Many saw his cure from leprosy as a miracle. 'I speak Lao, and those Lao settlers way over in the western jungles have never been reached with the Good News. Let's go!' Boon Mee's infectious enthusiasm led the missionary team into a new area and soon Lao, Thai and Karen people were worshipping God in the newly-planted little church in the remote hills.

The Uthaithani church groups began to appreciate Boon Mee's worth as a pastor and commenced giving him five dollars a month towards his support. But it was never easy. The Khonkaen Bible School had not given him specific pastoral training; and it was so hard for him with his disfigured face to stand confidently in front of people who'd never had leprosy. What a wonderful day when the leprosy doctor gave Boon Mee a new set of bushy eyebrows and the lay pastors' training school started in Uthai! Again Satan attacked. The churches, rather immature in their understanding of pastoral support, suddenly failed to contribute. At home, Chusee was poorly, pining for the baby that never arrived; his rice fields had been neglected; his health borderline. His own unfortunate weakness for buying deceased vehicles that refused to be resurrected didn't do anything to relieve the financial strain.

Suddenly he was offered a post as nightwatchman at Manorom Hospital. What a test of his commitment! After much heart-searching he decided God wanted him to continue as a pastor. He dumped the latest bomb, a black van, under a Christian charcoal seller's house and adopted a baby for Chusee. The very next month he felt that God had confirmed his call when three men came to Christ through his own outreach ministry and ten others were under real conviction. Best of all, he stood every month before a group of about twenty budding leaders from the little church groups dotted across Uthaithani province, taking his turn at teaching in the two-day lay pastors' training school, to which one man came seventy kilometres. Within a year or two his far-off district would have enough groups to warrant their own leadership training classes. As the men and women sat cross-legged on the floor behind the church benches which they used to write on, Boon Mee's heart rejoiced that at last in-service training was a reality. Neither he nor the missionary — and even he left in 1976 — could hope to travel to over twenty groups each Sunday. As on the second day the students constructed and practised sermons, and checked out their cassettes of music and teaching from the lending library, he knew they would not have to.

Boon Mee represents one tradition of leadership — the older man, paid little or nothing, who has spiritual maturity, understanding of the local church, and good standing in the community. But many potential leaders fell by the way, particularly those who did not have the regular spiritual support of the salas. Because the OMF work had tended to concentrate on the rural and poorer people in the community, the choice of leaders was limited. In the towns the Christians were often the peripatetics, students, and real or de facto widows. The middle class ones were victims of the seven-day-a-week rat-race of life, and leadership training had to be repeatedly resuscitated. Even in the country many potential leaders would suddenly disappear to work somewhere else or would find it impossible to withstand pressures crushing

them — a non-Christian wife, or a believing wife under the domination of unconverted relatives; and in Thai culture, the wife is traditionally the keeper of the purse. Taking time 'off' to work for the Lord when all were chronically poor often resulted in family upsets or financial want.

After fifteen years there were only two groups with elected leadership, and the missionary team felt that one of the reasons for this slow development was the lack of a daily 'quiet time'. The majority were indifferent readers with poor comprehension ability, and the advent of cassettophones in 1970 was a great boon, for they helped poor readers to meditate on the Word of God daily. Theological Education by Extension materials have been prepared, but are still too academic in format for the majority. Although the concept of lay pastors' in-service training seems to have been accepted since 1971, particularly where it is on a regional basis, the training of local leadership still needs more original and constructive thought. The latest innovation is an Open Bible School concept for higher level at-home study and practice for leaders.

At the same time a different but complementary type of leadership was emerging. In 1964 Mr Arphon was sent to the New Zealand Bible Training Institute for three years. His going reflected a need for intensive Bible education, but not many could have such an elite opportunity! OMF Central and North Thailand fields combined resources to build a residential Bible training centre on the slopes above the placid Phayao lake near Chiang Rai; it was opened by John and Muriel Davis in June 1966 with six students. Basic Bible truth was to be taught regardless of previous levels of education. At first it was envisaged that whole families would attend, like Samrit, from the Manorom carpentry department, who took along his plump wife, Green Lotus. But it was not an easy time for Green Lotus, with two little boys to care for and not really being part of the student group. Increasingly Phayao appealed to younger people, single men and girls with fewer family commitments. There was the added advantage of meeting keen young Christians who could be future marriage partners. Back home the likelihood of finding a Christian to marry was minimal.

1973 saw the first three of the zealous group of graduates daring to step out into districts unfamiliar to them in order to help the church, and in 1975 Bangkok Bible College graduates joined them. Growing pains there were aplenty. With no fields or Christian families to back them, they expected the still tiny church to support them adequately, even if they decided to get married during the time. The hazards were real. Giving, often erratic, might cease without warning, leaving the house rent unpaid and the young wife in a wallow of homesickness. Thai tradition is that young mothers work while the grandparents mind the babies; the young church worker's wife, miles away from relatives, faced many emotional upheavals, and might beg her husband to give up. He had his own worries too — the church elders regarded him as a youngster and did not fully trust him with management of the church, even though they hoped he would do all the work. Because the church was indigenous he was not responsible to the missionary team in the area and only took their advice if he felt like it. The situation needed clarifying, and by 1978 both Phayao and Bangkok Bible College had worked out one-year internship schemes which brought greater security to the young church workers by giving them a year's experience working with a local church or older colleague.

This gift of trained young men and women is of inestimable value to the Church in Central Thailand. From the first year some were elected onto the Central Churches Committee, acting as catalysts in the various programmes especially the regional youth and children's camps, bringing musical and communication improvements, and running several six-week Bible schools in Chainat town. Although some graduates have managed for a short time on their own, the most successful church workers are those who work in conjunction with a resident missionary, both benefitting from the spritiual encouragement and companionship.

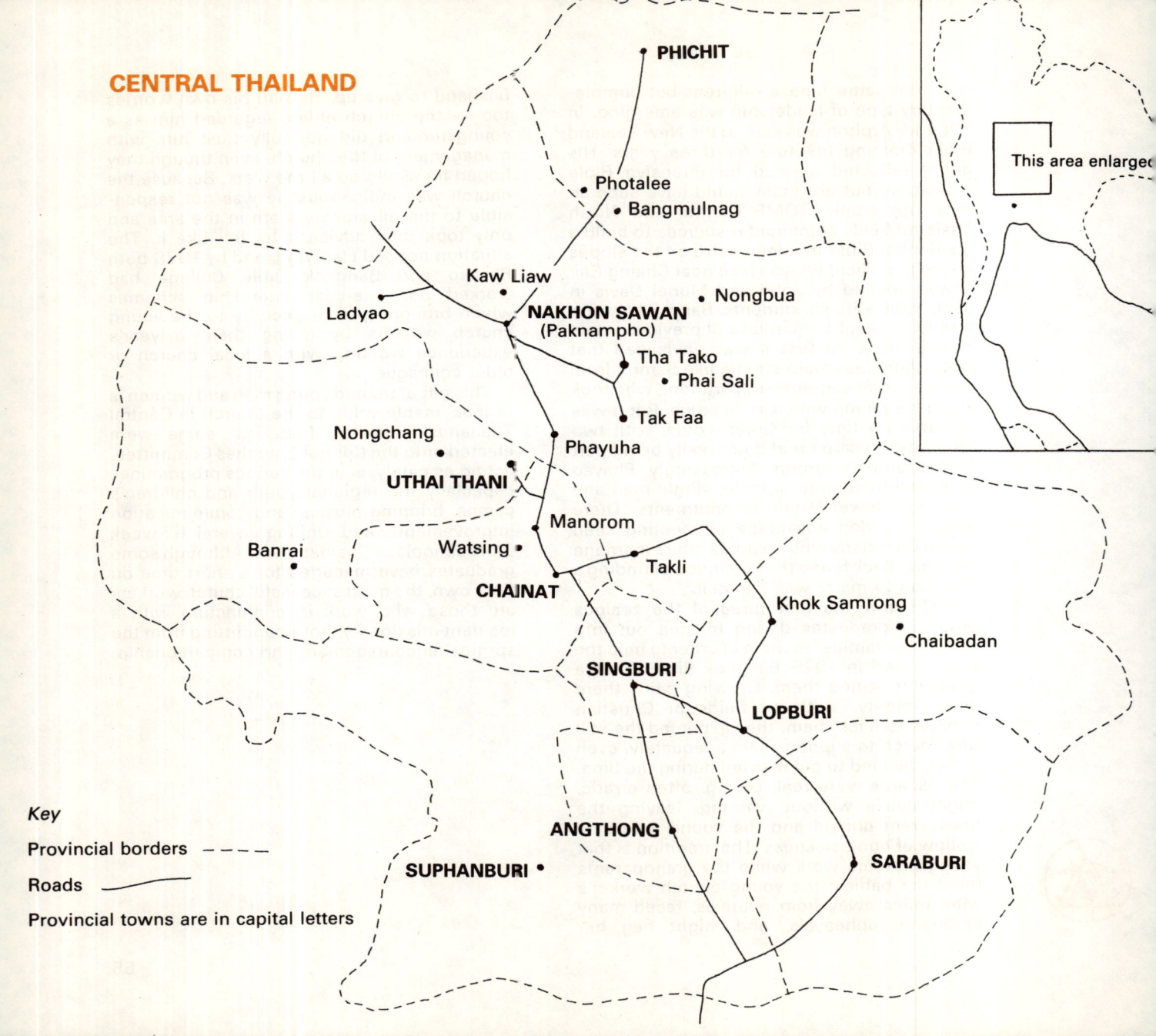

TO WIN OTHERS ALSO

Because the aim of the missionaries was 'the Gospel to every creature', and yet the first believers were in need of so much careful nurture, there only had to be two missionaries and two cups of coffee for a discussion to start. 'Should we concentrate on building up the Christians, or give everyone in our area an opportunity of hearing the Gospel first?' Most missionaries arriving from the West were well experienced in caring for Christians, and affected by the prevalent idea that East Asia only needed missionaries in supportive roles while the Asians reached one another for Christ. But the Central Thailand missionary was called to pioneer evangelism. Even in 1978, 850 Christians among five million needed help in reaching out to the unconverted.

During the 1950's and 60s many different methods of evangelism were tried. The Gospel launch travelled throughout the waterways but its activity was restricted more to the wet season, while farmers were freer in the hot dry season when the ground was like concrete, too hard to plough until the monsoons broke. So in 1958 a Land Rover fitted with loudspeakers and film equipment was purchased to speed the task of evangelism. Seed-sowing was boosted too by the advent of medium-wave commercial stations in 1964. Time was bought on four stations but registered response was meagre and when the rates went up in one centre the missionaries decided not to renew the contract. But the radio station itself received requests, and the programme was reinstated at the old rate! A Christian couple living next door to a temple heard the priests tuning every night to the Christian fifteen minutes' worth. Literature was used too, and OMF Publishers in Bangkok started a contest for young people. Local missionaries sold competition booklets through schools and gained increased contacts. The idea was so successful that the annual contest has continued to the present.

In 1966, a roving evangelistic team began to be used, with an elaborate mobile stage drawn by the Land Rover. Unfortunately, the trailer's narrow wheel base proved a bit of a practical liability! The variety programme was invited to supplement the efforts of small church groups in reaching out to their neighbourhood. The team itself felt the venture very worthwhile but the scheme lapsed after a year when not enough missionaries were available. Actual conversions reported were not impressive.

Intensive, large-scale campaigns were tried, such as at Sanburi where 60,000 tracts were distributed during pre-campaign visiting. Again the results were not spectacular — four men and eight young people believed, as well as fifteen children — as a result of the special children's meetings. Grace Harris, the children's evangelist, saw the necessity of adequately following up the young believers and started a children's camp. Camping was a revolutionary idea in 1968 but it was immediately acceptable, with 38 children at the first one. Numbers have grown each year since then and children who have made professions are followed up by personal letters and, if possible, holiday Bible schools in their area. The camps themselves provide valuable training in evangelism for young adults.

One campaign was a literature thrust, planned for the largest city in the region, Paknampho. Every home was visited, many twice or more, and a number started correspondence courses. One man wanted to believe but did not like to shame his family. He assured his mother he would not 'turn' until he

left to study in Europe. The local church did not see increased membership either from the thrust or from the emphasis on youth work at that time. Eighty students were attending the Sunday morning Bible Class, and half a dozen of them would engage in evangelism every Sunday afternoon. Even the Teachers' Training College had a small group meeting; and missionaries were teaching in the schools.

To undergird all this activity, and mobilise the Christians, Dr Toyotome of Japan was invited in 1966 to teach and see started the pattern of prayer cell evangelism which had been so successful in parts of Japan. But it was not easy to keep prayer cells functioning when members were scattered over a wide rural area.

The missionary team took stock of all the effort. There was fruit, but it was meagre. The enthusiasm of the team had to rely on faith in God rather than visibility of results. Said one, 'If God's Word is a hammer we need to keep hitting!' The years of discouragement and for many, illhealth, were nevertheless taking their toll and during the sixties the church-planting team was heavily depleted through the resignation of valued workers. One young couple arriving in Singapore asked to be sent to a difficult area for evangelism. 'Central Thailand!' the General Director answered

immediately, 'they're discouraged and haven't had a new couple in that work for four years.' As they disembarked at Bangkok two more Central Thailand couples were leaving. The new workers asked the Superintendent, 'What evangelistic methods are most successful with the Thai?' Everything had been tried, he answered, and nothing had really worked. The team was waiting for the Spirit of God.

By 1970 a note of optimism was creeping again into reports about Central Thailand; and that year the number of conversions was double that of any of the previous four years. The Thai Congress on Evangelism led to seminars on Church Growth and evangelism-in-depth techniques which had proved fruitful in other parts of the world. Up country a young couple were putting these techniques into practice.

After their return from their first furlough, Alex and Faith Smith were determined under God to break away from the now-less-fruitful routine of the evangelist working out from the leprosy clinics in Uthaithani province — Thai Christians should be able to carry that on. They were concerned that much of the province had never been reached with the Good News, and began extensive visiting in the western villages of the Ban Rai district. Here settlers were clearing the jungle for corn and upland crops, and travel in and out to their homes along the logging trails was rough. The missionary team often spent a week or more at a time living in the area, leaving their wives and children back in Uthai town. Gradually the more responsive villages were pinpointed. Evangelistic attacks were then planned for the long hot dry season when people came out after sunset to sample the entertainment offered. There's plenty: medicine sellers and temple fairs show films or hire professional actors. To take advantage of this opportunity, the mobile stage came out of mothballs and its deep red curtains were washed. Large groups of students from Phayao moved in to produce a varied programme appealing to all levels and ages.

But this was no entertainment — it was a battle between Christ and Satan. The team would be counselling at midnight, then visiting the same people in their homes the next day. If there were conversions, several students would stay behind, while the team moved on to the next village, to give help and teaching to the new Christians who were quickly exposed to a vicious power conflict. Other special emphases were the importance of winning key men or whole families, baptizing people soon after their conversions, starting Sunday services even where there were only two or three believers, and sending one from each group to the monthly lay pastors' training school which was by then developing. Bi-monthly regional conferences brought the little groups together to provide the desperately-needed fellowship.

Although Uthaithani led the way, other provinces were also searching out responsive pockets, nearly always rural, and seeing the believers strengthened immediately by the lay leadership practical training in which they learnt by doing not just listening. After five years the impact of this pattern of evangelism began to lessen as more extensive irrigation meant fewer farmers were free in the hot season; and the aging films and projector could not compete with the avalanche of new commercial films now available. But now there were Christians in these communities, who could reach out to others around them. But what about the unresponsive areas — the urban communities — the still unreached eastern part of the region? 21 of the 57 district towns in Central Thailand had no Christian

witness after 25 years. Yet these towns were the focal points for education, communications, government, business, machinery repair and marketing. A strategy must be found to see a church established in each one, which would eventually 'work' its own district. The team aim had already been stated in a more succinct way: 'a church in every community and thereby the gospel to every creature'. The team could not just wait for responsiveness; they decided to make half of the 21 communities targets for placement of personnel and evangelistic attacks.

The number of church-planting missionaries was hopelessly inadequate for the task. How could the challenge be met? Only, it seemed, by leaving still weak church groups to get along by themselves, proving their dependence upon God. But He had reinforcements ready. In 1977 the foreign missionaries' hands were strengthened by the formation of the Thai Home Missions Board, initiated from Phayao. The first two home missionaries, Phayao graduates who had already completed internship years, started in one of the district towns. They had the same burden and vision for these strategic centres. Nowhere was the new thrust and new partnership more clearly seen than at Tatago, one of the 21 towns.

One of the nurse-aides at Nongbua Christian Hospital was a bit of a troublemaker. She did not believe in God and did not intend to make it easy for the other girls to believe either. But one day Arirat found Christ as her Saviour. She was a clever outspoken girl, sometimes a bit too blunt, and when she went

home to her native Tatago an hour's journey away (if it didn't rain), she witnessed to her family and acquaintances. None believed but she was sure she'd made them start to think. Arirat appealed to the OMF Superintendent, Alan Bennett, 'Acharn ('teacher') Alan, you arrange for the placement of missionaries. Please send one to Tatago. There are so many interested people there. They would believe if only you could send someone.'

Alan told her that the team believed Tatago was a priority on two counts: it was both a district town and in the eastern part of the region. 'We tried it fifteen years ago, but we're willing to try again — if we can find workers!' 'Well, I'm praying for missionaries to go!'

Alan wrote to two missionary couples on furlough, one in Canada and one in England. Would they consider pioneering the Tatago-Phai Sali-Tak Fa area together? While there were flat stretches of rice paddy, the greater part was in upland scrub, corn or millet, with banditry after dark on the lonely roads. Both couples responded 'yes'.

Alan relayed the good news to Arirat. Excited! She was all for going out househunting right away! David and Jenny Robinson and Koos and Colleen Fietje moved in to Tatago in September, 1977. No church, no Christians. Their initial strategy was to make as many friends as possible while interest and curiosity in the newcomers were high. Every shopping and househunting trip became an opportunity for them to explain unhurriedly why they were living in Tatago. Because after three p.m. was when the most people were free to chat, they timed their trips accordingly. Within a few months the first had believed; and found it easy to make reciprocal calls at the missionary's shopfront home in the market. Within five months a weekly service had commenced, although individual teaching of believers continued as well as the efficient use of cassettes.

One of the neighbours of a new Christian was a fisherman, a wild character when indulging in his hobbies: drink, women and gambling.

He insulted his Christian neighbour as crudely as he knew how: 'Foreign dogs, that's what you are. Believing a foreign religion, you're just selling out your country! Communist!' There was nothing lower than a dog. If David or Koos called in, he sat and listened politely. Interested? Oh no! He was getting more ammunition to throw once the foreigners had left!

Slowly the same ammunition worked on him and he was conquered for Christ. There wasn't even time to tell him that drink, adultery and gambling were breaking God's laws before he announced, 'God through His Holy Spirit has told me that I must stop living the old life.' And stop he did. A few Sundays later a new lady showed up. 'Welcome, you are...?' 'I am the fisherman's wife. I want to know the power which changed this terrible man and gave me a new husband.' 'What?' called a lady who had overheard, 'You've got a new husband?' Marital scandal was a favourite conversation piece. 'Oh no! This is my old one but he's like a new one.' Husband and wife were both baptized on 15th April, 1979, along with 23 others. It was a day of great victory and rejoicing, with 75 young Christians publicly testifying to God's power. Most of them knew their new life would be challenged. Just an hour after the baptism one said, 'Teacher, that cross you said would come has already arrived. Pray for me'. Parades and other anti-Christian demonstrations were planned, and placards denouncing the baptisms pasted up.

David and Koos were staying away from home more and more nights in order to reach

each new believer personally with encouragement and teaching. Health and family life were suffering. They needed someone quickly who could build up the believers while they continued to spearhead the evangelistic outreach.

And God had someone ready. Wicharn and Oorai were Phayao graduates. Full of enthusiasm, they had gone to Angthong where the church was tiny and fellowship minimal. With no missionary anywhere near for sharing mutual concerns, loneliness and financial insecurity undermined their confidence and they withdrew, discouraged, to Oorai's non-Christian family home. While Oorai sold pomelos in a little stall outside Manorom Hospital, Wicharn managed lotus fields as a commercial venture. Had the Lord passed them by?

Then came the invitation to teach the believers of Tatago in a team ministry with Koos and David. They went with their two small children and are proving a tremendously effective part of the team.

Five outlying areas are being reached now and a second Thai couple, supported by the Thai Home Missions Board, have accepted the invitation to join the team.

Young Thai workers are very vulnerable when facing open ridicule or tackling heavy problems. The team ministry gives strength at these points. Practical problems are dealt with too. Koos has helped Wicharn to establish a chicken project as a means of income and respectability. One hundred egg-laying hens in neat coops proclaim that he is just another Tatago farmer and not merely a parasite on the foreigners! With over ten baptised couples now, the team is working to build the believers into a functioning church. In this the four young couples, two Thai and two from overseas, are looking confidently to the Lord of the harvest who sent them. Workers together for Christ!

Hudson Taylor's famous saying about work for God is an apt one for Central Thailand: 'I have found that there are three stages in every great work of God; first it is impossible, then it is difficult, then it is done.' There is a harvest but it is hard-won, with much ploughing, sowing and watering over many years. Central Thailand needs men and women who have an audacious faith in the Lord of the harvest, a faith that cannot be quenched.

QUESTIONS
1. 'All one in Christ Jesus', wrote Paul. Does this mean 'leprosy' and 'well' Christians should always worship together? What problems would this bring?
2. Can you identify some of the factors which have made church-planting in Central Thailand so slow and hard?
3. Can you answer Jean Anderson's question, 'However does leading terminally-ill patients to Christ significantly contribute to the OMF goal of planting churches in Central Thailand? What is needed if it is to do so?
4. What kind of leaders are most effective in rural areas like these, and how can they be trained? What problems will they meet?
5. How important is it for new Christians to feel part of a Christian community, especially if family or neighbours reject them? How can this be achieved?

SOUTH THAILAND

A START IN THE SOUTH

Laurie Wood and Gordon Aldis felt excited and full of anticipation as they set out for the South. They had heard about the four southern provinces with their large population of Muslims and had decided to go and see for themselves. The countryside was very beautiful, the people attractive, the dress eye-catching and the sea, with its fringe of golden sands and swaying palms was like something out of a travel brochure. But the hearts of the people living in that lovely part were dark and empty, for they knew nothing of the Lord Jesus Christ.

The two men returned with a report of wide-open doors, even among the Thai Muslims — often called Malays. After prayer and further preparation, a small team set off for this new field of work, and on the first of January 1953, Laurie Wood and his wife, with Dorothy Jupp and Doris Briscoe, moved into a house in the centre of Yala. As far as they knew there was only one Christian in the area, a young girl living in Betong, 85 miles to the south. Little did they know what lay ahead as three days later they sat on packing cases for their first Sunday service. To the curious passers-by their voices sounded feeble and inadequate, but there was nothing weak about the song they sang — 'Jesus the Name High over all.'

These missionaries had recently withdrawn from China and so were able to use Chinese in their initial outreach. They soon found that some of the Chinese shopkeepers had been Christians years before in China, but were no longer following the Lord. About this time several Christian families moved from Bangkok to Yala, drawn by the growing business generated by the rubber boom. They became the nucleus of what is today a church of some 60 members.

The aim of these first workers was to find areas where the people seemed to be responsive. But to do this they had to send feelers into the entire community. The largest group was the Malays who spoke their own dialect. Next in size came the Thai Buddhists, followed by the Chinese. Rubber plantations and tin mines were the main sources of employment, while fishing round the coast and coconut plantations brought in a living for many others. But which of this wide cross-section of society should they concentrate on? And which language should they try to learn?

Evangelism started almost immediately, with thousands of gospels and Scripture portions being sold at the weekly markets, and tracts in the various languages distributed throughout the towns and villages. Surveys were made of the different districts as more missionaries came to join the original band of four. Language study took up hours of time and most of the workers tried to get a grasp of both Thai and Malay — languages that are very different. But many an evening the books and tape-recorders were left and they joined in a new type of witness, often till well after midnight. Fairs are an integral part of life and culture of South Thailand. How the people love to flock to these brightly-lit, attractive displays of goods for sale. Lengths of brightly-coloured cloth, crystalised fruit and all sorts of sweet-meats, fried chicken with fiery curried sauce, as well as the 'fattest lady in the world', the 'two-headed monster' and a 'genuine man-eating tiger' — all for a few pence. It was to these fairs that the team went to give out literature and to shout as loudly as the next person — not to sell gaily-coloured sarongs or hot chicken legs, but to present to those swarming past the glorious message of the Lord Jesus Christ.

Quite soon a medical clinic was started.

Men and women began to see God's love demonstrated in living form to them — not just the printed word with its strange new teaching, but a loving, sympathetic concern for the whole man in all his spiritual need and physical sickness. Every effort to preach the Gospel was contested, but as the years went by the team began to see new believers in their ones and twos added to the small groups of Christians. The first baptisms were held on Christmas Day 1957, in Yala. Six new Christians witnessed to God's grace to them — one Indian, two Thai and three Chinese — and the only shadow to spoil that joyous morning was the fact that as yet not one Thai Muslim had responded to the Gospel. From that time the church grew slowly, and the first Believers' Conference was held in Yala in May 1959. From every centre Christians gathered to encourage each other in their joyful faith, and since then church conferences have been held annually in the Thai language in these four southern provinces.

CARE FOR THE SICK

Saiburi was chosen as the site for the Mission's main medical work in South Thailand. The Thai medical authorities had recommended it as a very needy area, and there was a large Muslim community, mostly consisting of fishermen. Since the Muslims were still proving resistant to the Gospel it was decided that Dorothy Jupp and Doris Briscoe would start a Gospel witness in the town to prepare the way for the medical workers, so the Christian clinic was opened in April 1955 in an old shop-front house on the main street. Three doctors, one nurse, a dispenser, registrar and evangelist came to man it. Western faces were still a novelty in those days and while many came for treatment others came just to stare at the strangers with their white faces, blue eyes and such long noses.

Gradually the Malay-speaking Muslims thawed and came to trust and love these people who cared for them and were so obviously interested in them. As the demand grew and greater numbers thronged to the clinic it was decided to open a small hospital. So, through prayer and the sacrificial giving of many at home, the Saiburi Christian Hospital was opened in 1960, amid the palms and beauty of the seaside. Almost from the very beginning crowds came to the Outpatients' Department, and this has continued to the present time with more and more coming each year. Others come for operations, or treatment requiring a stay of several days, and there are always some long-term patients. The hospital has won itself a reputation and people come from miles away because they know that they will be looked after with love and concern. Twice a week there is a service in the Outpatients' Department as Christian nurse-aides or other hospital workers join missionaries in singing and a short talk. Books are available to borrow or buy and each Christian on the staff is encouraged to witness to the patients as opportunity arises. Since there are people from both Malay and Thai communities this witness needs to be in both languages.

In 1963 it was decided that a leprosy treatment programme should be started, but it wasn't until 1966 that the first leprosy clinic was opened. Men and women already disfigured by the disease, and others afraid that their neighbours might learn of their condition, came to be cared for. Often the nurses had to visit patients in their homes because they were unable to get to the clinic themselves. One day, Brenda Holton was told of a poor Thai fellow who lived like a hermit in a broken-down hut, uncared for by his relatives or friends. When the nurses visited him he could hardly look at them, let alone speak to them, he was in such a pathetic state. As he heard the good news of the God of Heaven he turned in faith and became a Christian. Ten years later he had caught up on his education and been trained as a para-medic for the leprosy team. Such is the power of the Gospel.

Since treatment of leprosy takes months, or even years, patients hear the Gospel over a long period of time. This constant exposure to the message is the key to full understanding of its meaning. A wing specially built on to the hospital to provide for long-term patients who need specialized treatment, also provided the opportunity for constant teaching to a group of Malay men. And it was this same group who became the first true converts to Christ from among the Muslims in south Thailand, and who were baptized in 1973.

Because a missionary is surrounded on every side by tremendous needs and because several languages are used, there is the

tendency to try to do too much — but actually accomplish little. The tension of trying to use different languages is also great. So in 1972 the decision was made to divide the non-medical missionaries into two separate teams. Each missionary was asked to choose either the Thai team or the Malay team. He could then major on one religious background and concentrate on one kind of work. Objectives were drawn up and a strategy planned for each team. One of these objectives was long-term concentration on certain chosen areas — the hospital work had shown that when a patient was in hospital for a long period of time he was more likely to become a Christian. So it was decided to use this 'long-term' principle in the evangelistic work generally. In other words, there wouldn't be any more widespread scattering of the seed, but missionaries would spend longer on a smaller number of places.

The team, whether Thai or Malay, decides on a certain area. They visit in homes, give out tracts and show films in the open air. Then they will follow up any who show interest. This may mean loaning cassette tapes with recorded teaching, encouraging people to enrol in a Bible Correspondence course, or trying to start a house group with several neighbours in the hope that it will grow into a church.

Quite soon after the opening of the Saiburi Christian Hospital Mr Hok believed and received Christ. But he was the only Christian in his area. At first he was visited weekly and maintained his faith in Christ, though he did not openly witness to others. Later another man from the same area came to the hospital and he too believed. Alan and Maelynn Ellard felt the need to follow up Mr Hok and Mr Jie, so they began to visit in the Khuan area and give Bible teaching, and then to evangelize by house-to-house calls. After these initial visits they moved into Khuan village and began meetings in their home.

Through literature and open-air evangelism many more came to believe. Meetings were also held in the nearby Palas leprosy clinic. The believers were encouraged to attend a weekly meeting in Khuan for fellowship and worship. This meeting has now moved to nearby Dawn village; the Christians have bought their own piece of land and have erected a building for services which will eventually serve as a Pastor's house. Bible study meetings are held in various homes and stress has been laid on preparing leaders to carry on the work themselves.

CAN MUSLIMS BECOME CHRISTIANS?

The Malay team is in a very different situation because of Islam's opposition to Christian teaching. Muslims refute the fact that Jesus is God, that He died and rose again. In the early days when missionaries were widely scattered and isolated from one another, there was no response and the workers were discouraged. When the idea of teams was formulated the main emphasis was put on Pattani province and the area in and around Yala town.

Because of this opposition to the Gospel in Muslim villages, the Malay team's strategy had to be different from the Thai team's. It is always suspect when a missionary goes to visit Muslim people in their homes. Ostracism and threats will soon cause a person to lose interest. It is better to bring people in to a non-hostile environment. So, after much prayer and discussion, it was decided to open a house in Saiburi which could be used as a base for patients and visitors passing through. Here they could receive concentrated Bible

teaching. Another factor which led to the breakthrough among the Muslims was the change to the use of the local dialect, Pattani Malay. For years, missionaries had spent long tedious hours trying to learn standard Malay, which is spoken in Malaysia but is hardly used in South Thailand. A language course was produced in this local dialect, and now the translation of the New Testament is nearly completed.

It was like a dream come true when the first five Malays were baptized in 1973. It had taken 20 years of painstaking work — preaching, teaching, praying and caring. And when the day finally arrived it seemed unbelievable. How many servants of God had been involved in that final 'firstfruit' is impossible to measure. Many workers had come and gone, some because of ill-health, others discouraged by the hardness of the work. And hundreds in various countries had played the vital part in praying. All had shared in the emergence of this small church. One particular book used by God to bring about the conversion of these men was written by a Japanese Christian, Dr Toyotome. It takes the reader through the way of salvation and ends with a prayer of repentance and turning to Christ.

Since 1973 others have taken the step of baptism and a number are very interested in the Gospel. It is mostly fear that holds them back. The Malay Centre in Saiburi is a focal point for teaching and instructing the new believers, and cassettes have had a great contribution in this too — they are loaned to interested people and to those attending the hospital and leprosy clinics.

Early in 1976 a plan was drawn up to reach the Malays in the area around Yala. David Strachan and Bob Joyce selected 20 villages for intensive evangelism through tracting and

visits. After the initial visit the number of villages was reduced to twelve. These were then visited approximately every three to four weeks for almost a year with a different set of tracts on each occasion. Every opportunity was taken to talk personally with the villagers on the content of the literature. When a real interest was noticed, cassettes were loaned. Following this the five most sympathetic villages were chosen for three-night campaigns featuring films, filmstrips, preaching and testimony. This resulted in a dwindling of interest in two, but an encouraging response in the others. Further follow-up was continued in these, and the following year more campaigns held in them. So far as we know no one has yet turned to the Lord, but it is felt that this concerted and continuous evangelism enables people to understand the Gospel and encourages them to turn to Christ in groups. Furloughs, lack of personnel etc. are greatly hampering the continuing of this thrust.

SEED IN THE SOIL

There are various methods of reaching men and women for Christ, but God may sometimes allow a method that to our finite eyes seems completely 'way out'. Minka Hanskamp and Margaret Morgan, two of the leprosy team, were kidnapped one morning just as they arrived to hold a clinic. Shock waves reverberated through our immediate Mission family and through our wider circle of praying friends. Their kidnapping was soon followed by a demand note for ten million baht (about £250,000) along with demands of a political nature. Months passed. Hours were spent in prayer, in seeking to make contact and in negotiations. We hoped that the kidnappers would realise we would never meet their demands, and would then release the ladies. But no — their bodies were found nearly a year after their capture.

Pok Su, one of the first group of Malays to be baptized, gave a moving testimony at the funeral service. He said: 'It was when I saw my filthy, ulcerated foot held gently in her loving hands that I began to understand something of the love of God in sending Jesus Christ to die for me.' It would be gratifying to be able to say that through their deaths the Malay church has gone from strength to strength, but we cannot yet say this. However, the Malay church is growing, even though slowly, and it is true that through their deaths we have freedom to go on preaching and proclaiming the Gospel. It has helped the local people, both Thai and Malay, to see that there really must be something in what is being proclaimed.

QUESTIONS

1. South Thailand is an area of natural scenic beauty and attractive people. In what ways are the people empty and in need?
2. The Muslim population was suspicious of the foreigners. What was used to overcome this suspicion? What other means might have been used?
3. Why was the work of the Ellards in the Khuan area effective? What were the main points of their strategy?
4. How important is it to have the New Testament translated into every language and dialect? Can a church be planted using a New Testament in a 'second language'?

BANGKOK

THE HUB OF THE NATION

In the thinking of many Thai people, their country consists of two parts: Bangkok and 'up-country'. Bangkok is the metropolis where four and a half million people live and work. It is the centre of Government, the hub of business life and the only sea port of any size. It is the place to which millions of people have drifted in search of work, lured by the stories of money to be made and pleasures to be enjoyed. In spite of four-lane roads and overpasses, traffic jams exist in some parts for most of the day and evening. Originally the city was 90% Chinese, but other groups have moved to the hub of the nation from north, south, central and northeast Thailand, as well as from Burma, Cambodia and Laos.

When OMF was invited to commence work in Thailand, the aim was to go to places where no other groups were working. Since there were Presbyterian, Baptist and independent churches already established in the city, the Fellowship placed workers only to cover the specific needs of an office and a Guest House for those travelling in and out of the country. In due time a Study House was added, and later still a language laboratory. The burden to produce and distribute Christian literature led to the starting of OMF Publishers. Those who worked in these places lent their efforts to existing Thai and Chinese churches in the city.

OMF missionaries noted that one of the problems in the up-country churches was the mobility of students. Only a short time after becoming Christians, many of them left the rural areas to continue their education in the capital. So in 1963 a student contact centre was established as an experiment, to cater for their needs, and six years later Bill Merry and Andrew Way opened a student hostel close to one of the busy shopping areas. 'Makasan Palace', as it was affectionately called, had its own identity as a student hostel and was a place where young men grew in their Christian lives, becoming witnesses and workers in the churches and on college campuses.

Back in 1966 Mike and Joan Richards left the busy work in the Pharmacy Department of Manorom Christian Hospital to take up a lecturing post at Chulalongkorn University in Bangkok, with the express purpose of encouraging Christian students to meet in cell groups on campus, to witness, to produce literature and organize camps. Now Thai Christian Students has affiliated groups in nine colleges and universities and in twelve high schools, with four Thai workers supported mainly by Thai churches and graduates.

OMF had started the Phayao Bible Training Centre (in North Thailand) in 1966, but the conviction persisted that Bible training on a higher level was needed. Discussions with the Christian and Missionary Alliance culminated in the starting of Bangkok Bible College, jointly sponsored by the two missions. Dr Henry Breidenthal was transferred to Bangkok to head this up. Numbers of students have increased to 40, and the leadership of the college passed to Rev Timothy Jeng in 1978.

During late 1971, Bill Merry and Henry Breidenthal started a Sunday evening service at the Makasan student hostel, preceded by street preaching in the area. Though the response was small, a large step of faith had been taken. A few months later, on New Year's Eve, five OMF missionaries and seven young Thai Christians met to pray at Bangkok Bible College. Most of these Thai men lived in the hostel or in other missionary households, and

they committed themselves to God for whatever He would have them do in the coming year.

Seth, Somporn and Bill Merry agreed to rise early each morning to pray together in the hostel where they lived. After six weeks they were convinced that God was leading them to start a morning service in that hostel. So on February 13, 1972 a worship service was begun, marking the beginning of what grew into Makasan 'New Life' church. Three Thai men and the two OMF missionaries worked together in leading the church. The growth story revolved around conversions, frustrations and victories. New converts faced the obstacles of parental opposition, social persecution, temptations and depression. Significantly, many of those won to Christ were the friends and personal contacts of new believers, and many were young people from Chinese families. Some came through direct evangelism by Thai Christians or missionaries. Some of the new workers still in language study contributed to the momentum of evangelism and personal teaching. About half the members were won from Buddhism, the other half transferred from other churches, mainly up-country.

At the first worship service, Miss Surirat became a Christian. A month before she had been wandering in Lumpini Park, in the centre of Bangkok, her heart in a turmoil as she was torn between prostitution and suicide. In the park on that same afternoon was Miss Datchani, a student of Bangkok Bible College. She was drawn to the lonely, dejected Surirat

and explained the Gospel to her. This encounter led to new life in Christ and, despite ups and downs, she became an ardent spreader of the message. The sharing atmosphere and kind attitudes of the church members at Makasan provided the spiritual strength that Suritat needed.

Miss Sawalak was in her first year at university when a friend invited her to go to church. She was not really interested but felt obligated by the friendship, so went along. The prayers and earnestness of the older Chinese Christians deeply impressed her, though she hardly understood a word they said. The friend suggested they go that evening to hear a foreign preacher, Dr Henry Breidenthal. In response to the preacher's invitation, she and her friend received Christ as their personal Saviour. Sawalak came from a rather poor family, and though still young in her faith she trusted God to provide the finances for her education. He answered her prayers, and she completed her university course free of debt.

Some of the new converts lacked deep roots in the Word of God and turned back. Others gradually slid from a close walk with Christ. Nevertheless the Lord continued to add to the church, often using very ordinary people. In the midst of one of her spiritual downs, Surirat brought Toom to Dorothy Mainhood's house. That very night Toom humbly received Christ as her Saviour. Next day she returned to the factory where she worked and began to witness to her friends. Another girl came to Christ and then she in turn won another. The Holy Spirit used this chain reaction of friend-ship to win a number of young people. During the first year, twenty new converts were baptized and added to the church. So many were introduced to new life that the name of 'Makasan Palace' was changed to the 'House of New Life' in November 1972.

A rapid expansion of this new church inevitably led to growing pains. Yet the desire to share their faith spurred the members to reach out to other areas with the Gospel. Soon the Makasan meeting room was too small to accommodate the crowd of 70 who gathered. As they prayed, an idea was injected into their thinking — divide the membership and start a new church somewhere else.

Soon after this, missionary Mary Cooke witnessed to a taxi driver. He and a friend went to Makasan church, and later members visited the two men in their homes. In time both their families turned their lives over to Jesus Christ. Other families who lived nearby also seemed open to the Gospel. God was evidently leading to begin a new outreach in their area of Suan Plu, on the south side of Bangkok. In December 1974, one of the few older members, who had dedicated her purse as well as her life to the Lord, helped find a suitable house in the Suan Plu area. Fifteen of the members from Makasan transferred their membership and the second 'New Life Church' came into being.

The influence of OMF Publishers also had a crucial part to play in the partnership of bringing members into this church. Through Bill Wilson's vision, Gospel advertisements were regularly placed in Thai newspapers and magazines. Twenty-two year old Mr Thanee read one of these in a newspaper and wrote off for a free booklet. Still he was not satisfied — he wanted to know whether God was real. OMF Publishers sent him another booklet, the story of Victor Landero, a Columbian whose life was dramatically changed by the power of Jesus Christ. He read the booklet and wondered if God could change his life too. A few days later he received an invitation to

attend the Suan Plu church. After some indecision he finally went and met one of the leaders, Mr Prasert, who promptly led him to Christ. Thus in God's timing, two years of contact with the Gospel culminated in Thanee's conversion.

Like many thousands of other country people, Mr Bung came to seek work in Bangkok. He tried a number of jobs but none lasted very long and he finally returned home and entered the Buddhist priesthood. After a year he was still unsatisfied, so he decided to lay aside the saffron robes, leave the temple and seek another job in a factory. His confusion grew and he began to contemplate suicide. Then he read the Gospel advertisement in the newspaper, 'Come to me, all who labour and are heavy laden, and I will give you rest.' He cut out the advert and kept it for many weeks. Finally he decided to write in for the free literature offered. Books were sent and letters invited him to attend Suan Plu church. Eventually he went, and three Sundays later accepted Christ.

When Mr Mana came to work as a printer at OMF Publishers he was not a Christian. At first he opposed the Gospel. Unruffled, the Christian staff made friends with him and prayed for him. Before long he began attending church, was converted and became an active member of the church and was recently married in it.

Partnership in planting the church has many interesting aspects. For example, several years ago Mr Narong was driving along the Asian Highway with a friend when they had a terrible accident. The friend was killed outright and Mr Narong was taken to Manorom Christian Hospital with a broken limb. The Christian staff witnessed to him daily and he became a Christian. When he returned to Bangkok he linked up with Suan Plu church.

Since the Communist take-over of Indo-China in 1975, many refugees from Cambodia, Laos and Vietnam have fled to Thailand. They are placed in refugee camps and gradually processed for migration to other countries. So there is a constant flow through the Transit Centre, which is in Suan Plu. Mrs Pranee, a member of the Suan Plu Church, has worked full time with the Lao refugees along with Alice Compain. They encourage those who understand Thai to attend the church.

Several of those who were students at the Makasan hostel and were involved in the church there from the beginning, went on to receive theological training. Chungseng studied at Bangkok Bible College from the first year it opened. Then in 1973 Seth went to Singapore to study at the Discipleship Training Centre. When he returned in January 1976 it was evident that another move forward was imminent. Six months later the Makasan church agreed to open a new centre, across the Chao Phaya river in Dao Khanong district with Chungseng as the leader. A group from Makasan moved their membership with him and became the nucleus for this new church.

Meanwhile the Christians from Suan Plu church became interested in another new area — that of Satupradit, further east from them. Miss Wanni, the full time lady worker, visited and taught in homes in that district and members went out in teams on Sunday afternoons. At the same time, a Thai student at Monash University in Australia became a Christian through the Overseas Christian Fellowship there. Mr Kriengsak was concerned that his family at home in Bangkok hear this same message, so the OMF Australian home staff wrote to Alex Smith, asking him to visit Kriengsak's family in the Satupradit area. In February 1977 Kriengsak came home for a holiday. The very first

evening back he led his two sisters to the Lord and next morning took his whole family to the Suan Plu church.

Only a week before, Pastor Seth had opened the new centre at Satupradit. In God's divine plan this was at the other end of the street from where Kriengsak's family live. Again, partnership in the Gospel was used to bring the first converts into this new church. The sisters were baptized along with eleven other new converts in June 1977.

OMF's partnership in church planting in Bangkok may be compared to changing gears in a car. In first gear OMF assisted others in already existing churches. With the development of the 'New Life Churches' came the change into second gear. Now that these churches have gained their own identity, OMF prepares to move into third gear. Many areas of Bangkok still have no churches. Vast sections of the city's four and a half million people remain unevangelized. Partnership with others will continue, but also in obedience to the command of the Lord Jesus Christ, the Gospel is being shared and new churches begun.

QUESTIONS

1. If a Christian goes to live in a city where there already are several churches, what should determine whether he works with one of these existing churches, or aims to start a new one?
2. The Makasan church began when Thai Christians and missionaries met together for prayer. How important is it to involve national Christians from the very beginning of a new work? What should a missionary do when there are no Christian in his area?.
3. At what stage in the development of a local church should it consider dividing to start a new church? Could this method be used here at home?
4. One of the key factors in the growth of the New Life churches has been the 'chain-reaction of friendship'. How does one get such a chain-reaction started?

NORTH THAILAND

North Thailand presents a challenge to Christian missions as formidable as its great mountain ranges, as diverse as its many peoples and languages and as tough as any pioneer area in the world. Dr McGilvary began work among the northern Thai in 1867 and today more than half the Christians in Thailand live in the north. But for many years the animist tribal people were neglected by Christian missions. Some outreach was made to the Karen and Lahu, but it was not until the 1950s that there was a planned approach to reaching the 250,000 or more tribal people scattered across the 42,000 square miles of rugged mountains.

CIM missionaries who had previously worked among the tribes of southwest China were delighted to find the Lisu, Lahu and Meo and to be introduced to new groups like the Yao, Akha and Karen. It was a happy sight to see the familiar tribal dress and their expectations were high. They had seen God work mightily among the Lisu of Yunnan province in China; they were fluent in the language and already had a wealth of knowledge about Lisu culture; they were used to living in remote, rugged conditions; and they had faithful prayer supporters who shared with them in prayer for the Lisu church in China and Burma as well as for this new advance.

The pioneers who moved to Thailand after the exodus from China had deep impressions of the Communist takeover. How long would Thailand remain free? Would they be evacuating yet again within a matter of years? These fears increased their desire to get on with the job and were a sustaining motive through the years of learning new dialects or languages. They knew from experience in China that only a church with the Bible in its own language could hope to stand after missionaries were forced to leave. And they wanted to plant churches which would maintain the traditional patterns of tribal culture and leadership. So after a time of exploratory trekking, consultation with other missions and discussion and prayer, the pattern emerged and OMF took on responsibility for the Akha, Lisu, Blue and White Hmong, Yao and Pwo Karen as well as the Shan people (an ethnic group related to the Thai, rather than a tribe). For some time OMF also worked among the Lahu but this was later handed over to another mission; and more recently work has been begun among the Sgaw Karen.

Especially during the last decade, the tribal situation in Thailand has been rapidly changing. The government is taking a much greater interest in the tribal people, seeking to give them agricultural, medical and educational help. Buddhism is being promoted as a means of encouraging integration into Thai society. New roads are constantly being made which increase the accessibility of many villages. To their dismay tribal leaders are seeing their cultural patterns crumbling. More and more tribal people are travelling freely among the Thai and many are moving down from the mountains to settle in the plain. Young people are being educated in Thai. Radios are bringing new ideas even into remote villages. We are finding more and more tribal people ready to trust in Jesus Christ, and church planting has accelerated steadily over the past five or six years.

QUESTIONS

1. What did the missionaries from China see as the most important job to be done when they moved to the tribes of north Thailand?
2. Why must a missionary learn the language of a tribe? Wouldn't the national (or trade) language be good enough?

AKHA

There are about 10,000 Akha scattered over the mountains along the borders with Burma and Laos. They are looked down upon as the most dirty and degraded of the tribes, but although poor and despised they are actually a lovable people. Their navy skirts, brightly decorated jackets, knee-length leggings and cone-shaped hats decorated with monkey fur and silver identify an Akha woman anywhere. They are steeped in animism and appear satisfied with their own complicated culture

and society — though less so than they once were.

Peter and Jean Nightingale were the first missionaries to try to reach the Akha in Thailand. They longed and prayed for an opportunity to live among them, but were never given permission to build a house within the demon gates which form the entrance to every heathen village. For six years they lived in a Thai village in the foothills, making trips up to the Akha villages and learning their language.

Peter and Jean shared their excitement with their praying friends at home — 'a young Akha couple who are Christians have come across from Burma to witness to the Akha in Thailand'. Surely God was at work — there must be a turning to Christ soon. Ya ju and his wife wanted to live in a heathen village, make their own fields and tell their neighbours what Christ meant to them. It took quite a lot of persuading, but finally the leaders of Khayeh village in Chiang Rai province gave grudging permission. Soon it became apparent that Ya ju and his wife were not going to take part in the village demon worship. The villagers were naturally suspicious. They listened to what the couple had to say but few showed any interest.

One man believed, but soon afterwards he was blamed for the sickness of a relative and turned back after being beaten up by the demon priest. Another family wanted to believe, but no sooner had they talked of it than their old father died and they were engulfed in demon ceremonies.

By the end of five years, Ya ju and his wife were desperate. Surely they had come in response to God's call. Why then had He let them down like this? One of their children had died, their rice crop had been burned, there was the constant jeering and open hatred of the other villagers and, worst of all, no one had stood as a Christian. What was the use? They might just as well return to their home in Burma. They cried to God to show them what to do, and pleaded yet again for some Akha to turn to Christ. Unknown to them, the missionaries spent their end-of-year Day of Prayer likewise pleading with God for a breakthrough among the Akha.

Within a couple of weeks, four men took a firm stand for the Lord, followed soon after by a fifth. The inevitable storm of opposition, threats and illness broke upon them, but they stood firm. So in desperation the villagers threw them out. It was a bitter blow, but the Lord gave them fresh courage and they set about building a new village not far away. Here at last was a place where missionaries were welcome to build a house and live among the Akha Christians.

Slowly the group grew as others came to join them. Ya ju realized that it was important to set a high standard of morality, so strict discipline was emphasized. He also taught them hymns in their own language which were used across in Burma, and got copies of the newly-translated Akha New Testament. Those who could not read were taught, and worship services contained regular Bible-based sermons.

So strong is the community spirit among the heathen villages that anyone who wants to become a Christian is forced to leave and go and live in a Christian village. So the Christians tithe their rice in order to support these new families for the first year until they can get their own harvest.

After some time, Ya ju went to work with a family planning scheme and was away from home for most of his time. But this also worked for the advance of the Gospel, because it gave him opportunities to visit all the Akha villages in Thailand, and he was able to spend the

evenings in personal witness and evangelism. As a result of this and of the witness of others, twelve new Christian villages have come into being.

These new Christians needed teaching in the faith and help in learning to read. Teachers were needed, but where could they be trained? Several had tried studying at Phayao Bible Training Centre — one had been there for two years — but they found studying in Thai too hard and finally gave it up. So a month-long Rainy Season Bible School was held in 1974 using the Akha language. It was later that year that the first large group of Akha turned to Christ — a whole village believed en bloc — and in the same year too that the first teachers were sent out, fully supported by the Christians to whom they ministered.

What caused these large-scale 'turnings'? One of the chief attractions of Christianity is the help given with breaking the opium habit, and the consequent better standard of living. Motives such as these brought trouble in the years ahead.

In 1976 tragedy struck the first Christian village, Elephant Valley, when the village was burnt down and the Christians lost their homes, their belongings and their rice. The few who didn't lose everything showed brotherly love and shared their homes and food with those who did. Swiss Christians sent large gifts to help rebuild the village, buy more rice and replace lost possessions. Was the fire a plot by nearby villagers to force the Akha Christians to move? If so, it failed and the church continued to grow.

In the battle for the souls of men, the devil has many different ways of fighting. Direct opposition and great suffering failed to shake the Akha Christians from their faith. Next he moved against the missionaries. Peter and Jean Nightingale were forced home by ill health. Peter underwent surgery and return to full-time work in Thailand was out of the question. However, he was able to visit Thailand for an Akha leaders' conference in February 1977, after which he wrote, 'Returning after one year away, I sense the pace of turnings quickening, the Akha church's response rising to the challenge. I feel the church stands on the verge of some large turnings, some blessed "refreshing" and some vicious attacks by the enemy.'

Barely a month later, fellow-missionary Peter Wyss and a Swiss friend were brutally murdered along the trail to Maeha village. Peter's wife Ruth and two other lady missionaries, together with the Akha teachers, bravely carried on with the month-long Bible School they had been preparing for. Ruth later returned to Switzerland to care for her three children.

Four missionaries (two of whom focus primarily on agricultural help) continue in partnership with the Akha leaders. At present all the trained leaders live in one village, Elephant Valley, and the other Christian villages desperately need teaching to bring them from their rather nominal faith to a true commitment to Christ.

QUESTIONS
1. How important is it actually to live among a group of people in order to witness to them, rather than simply to visit them from a base elsewhere?
2. What special part did prayer have in winning the first Akha to Christ? Is there a lesson here for us in our daily witness to non-Christian friends?

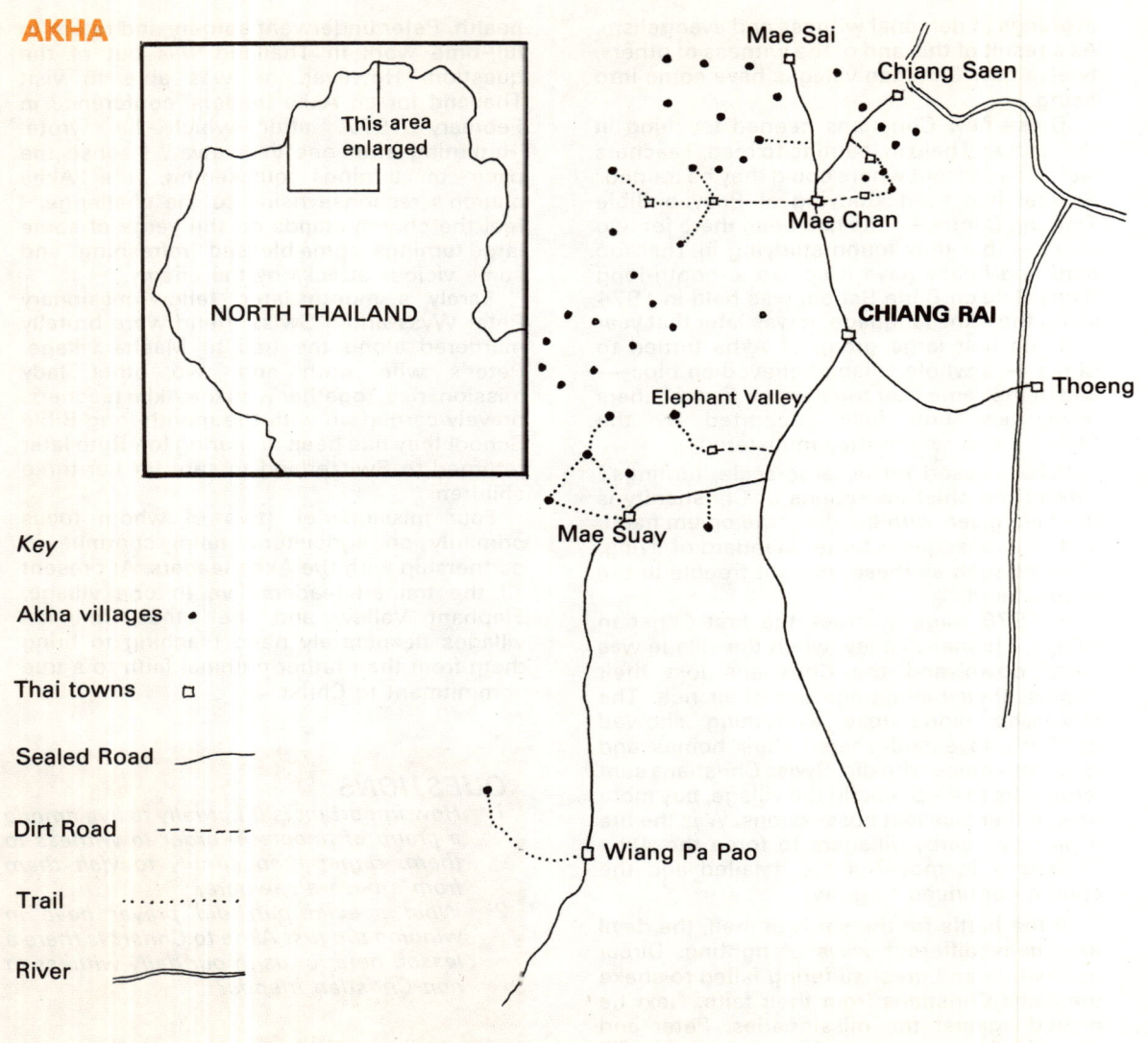

THE LISU

Probably the best known and most loved of the tribes in Thailand, as a result of Isobel Kuhn's books, the Lisu are an industrious people with strong roots back to China. Their wide turbans and blue and green dresses with rows of colourful trimming make the Lisu women conspicuous and very photogenic.

An enthusiastic start was made among the Lisu, but ill health limited the amount of time the first missionaries could spend up in the tribal villages. They also discovered that there are considerable differences between the dialect of Lisu they knew from China and the dialect spoken in Thailand. New missionaries joined the work and they learned the local dialect, so fear and suspicion gradually vanished.

There was great excitement and keen anticipation when four Lisu evangelists came over from Burma, where there are large numbers of Lisu and strong churches. The preachers visited Lisu villages for three months, explaining the Gospel and what it meant to become a Christian, but there were no lasting results. As recently as 1966 there were no Lisu Christians in Thailand.

In 1967 an influential young man named Benno decided to break from demon worship and become a Christian. But no one else would join him and for three years he remained the one lone believer. Eventually, three couples in the village of Rice Fields who were related to Benno turned to Christ. On Easter Sunday 1970, the small group was baptized. Sadly, Benno refused baptism and has now drifted away from the Lord.

Word spread across the mountains from village to village. 'Some of the Lisu of Rice Fields village have left the ancient ways and now worship a new God. They claim that He protects them and their crops.' Intrigued to know more, two men from Huay Hu village walked for a day and a half to visit the Christians and found that they were their relatives! They and their families left the demon way and committed their lives to Christ. They found that Jesus did indeed help them and when one of them became ill, they prayed and he was healed. The non-Christian Lisu were amazed and three more men believed.

Two Lisu Christians from Burma, Moses and Titus, heard of the new Christians in Thailand and moved across with their families to live in Rice Fields. The Christians built their own church building and men went out with Moses and Titus preaching in other Lisu villages. New Christian groups were begun in Fish Bone Creek and Elephant Mountain. Literacy classes were taught and Gospel Recordings made for use in witnessing. One man set the Gospel to music, using the traditional Lisu chants, and non-Christian Lisu readily listened to these. By 1974 all the groups had grown and the largest, Rice Fields village, had 41 baptized members.

Unfortunately, all the OMF Lisu workers moved to other work, but other missions maintained a link with the Rice Fields church. Retired CIM-OMF Lisu workers, the Cookes and the Cranes, have made visits to Thailand and held a six-week Bible School. Then in 1978 Andrew Thomson was designated to work among the Lisu. He plans to concentrate on Bible teaching and leadership training once he learns the language. Now he lives in Rice Fields village and works closely with Paul, one of the church leaders.

LISU

QUESTIONS
1. What helped to overcome the fear and suspicion of the Lisu?
2. Of what special significance do you think were the Gospel songs set to traditional Lisu chants? How important is it to find indigenous poetry, music and other art forms for worship and evangelism? Might there also be some dangers with such music? What dangers?

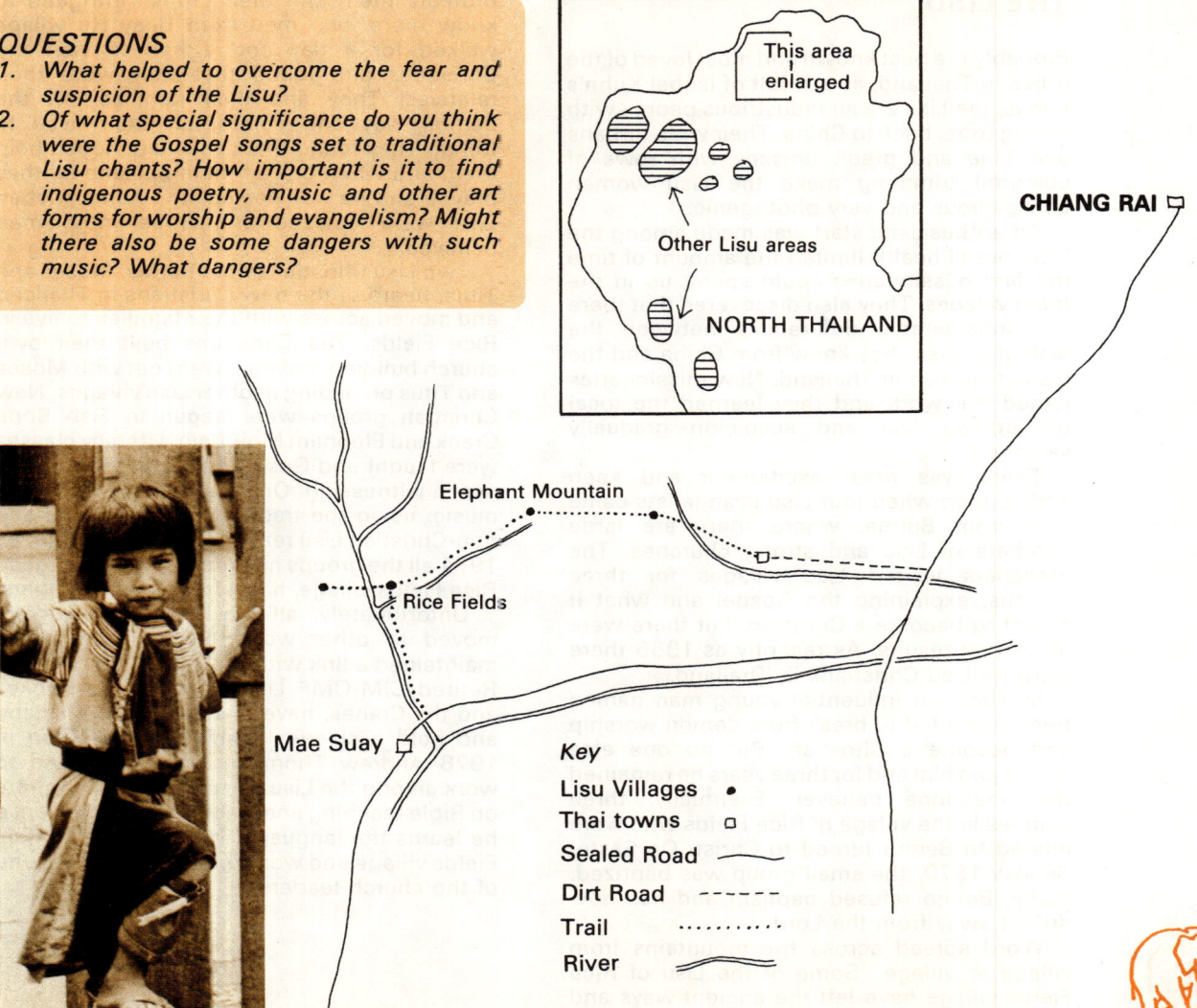

Key
- Lisu Villages ●
- Thai towns ▫
- Sealed Road ———
- Dirt Road - - - - -
- Trail ....
- River

THE YAO

Altogether there are thought to be between a half and one million Yao scattered across southern China, Burma, Vietnam, Laos and north Thailand. They are a vigorous, hard-working people whose consuming passion is the accumulation of wealth and the security it brings. They worship their dead ancestors and a hierarchy of powerful spirits. They are extremely individualistic and often live in isolated field houses growing rice, opium, red peppers, maize, soya beans and peanuts.

Lack of suitable mountain slopes is now forcing a steady movement to the plains, which in turn is causing an increasing assimilation of Thai culture, particularly among those of the younger generation who attend Thai schools. This is in contrast to the older people, many of whom can read and write Chinese. Their ritual songs use a language related to Chinese and their spirit worship is conducted in that language.

The first Yao in Thailand to become a Christian was the wealthy and influential headman of Maesalong village, called Brother Six. Allyn Cooke doggedly slogged up the steep muddy trail eighteen times before Brother Six finally took a stand for Christ. But when he did believe, most of the village joined him. Eric and Helen Cox moved into the village the following year to reduce the Yao language to writing and provide literature, and to teach the new Christians. Literacy classes were taught five days a week and a simple translation of Scripture verses was made for use in Sunday services. The Yao Christians constructed a simple bamboo and thatch church with earth floor and wooden benches.

It had been agreed that new converts must first break with smoking, growing and trading in opium before being eligible to receive baptism. So it was five years before the first Yao were baptized. This highlights what has been a constant problem for the tribal people. The great hold that opium smoking has over many of them and the ease with which money

can be made through selling it have been the cause of many remaining weak in the faith.

Many of the one thousand Yao in the area around Maesalong heard the Gospel during the first seven or eight years. Some were bitterly opposed and moved away to escape from Christian influence and to hold on to the traditional way. But in subsequent years, missionaries would often find friendliness and hospitality in some far-off village and trace it to someone who had moved from the Maesalong area.

Brother Six and several of his relatives moved to the market town of Maechan to match their business skill against that of the Thai and Chinese. Other families established a new village in the foothills east of Maechan, calling it Nongwaen. Gway Seng took on the leadership of this church. Large numbers of Yao professed conversion, particularly when Brother Six and John Davis (a northern-Thai speaking missionary) trekked over the hills together, visiting Yao villages and preaching. By 1966 the total Christian community stood at 500 in 17 villages, but only 84 of these had been baptized. The Yao were happy to be delivered from the oppressive burden of the ancestral spirits, but they never seemed to develop into mature Christians capable of leading responsible local churches. Materialism, gambling and opium seemed greater influences in their lives than the Lord Jesus or the desire to win others for Him. Few bothered to learn to read and lack of follow-up teaching left many at a shallow level of faith.

There was a desperate need for well-trained leaders who could teach their own people and lead them on deeper with the Lord. Two Yao men attended Phayao Bible Training Centre, but few of the Yao had a high enough standard in the Thai language to benefit from study there. What was needed was a course of study in Yao.

In an attempt to meet this need, three-week Leadership Training Schools were held for two successive years and these grew into a small Yao Bible School. David Griffiths compiled a course around the doctrine of the church, relating theology and church history to what the Yao need to know to function as individual Christians and in relation to one another in the church. This programme has continued for several years and has proved to be most worthwhile. The biggest problem however is the small number of Yao who can read sufficiently to benefit from the course.

To tackle this problem, a set of Reading Primers was produced. Workshops were held to train teachers to use the books. At about the same time, the long-awaited translation of the New Testament came from the printers and new readers were able to read the Word of God in their own language at last.

Steady numerical growth continued and

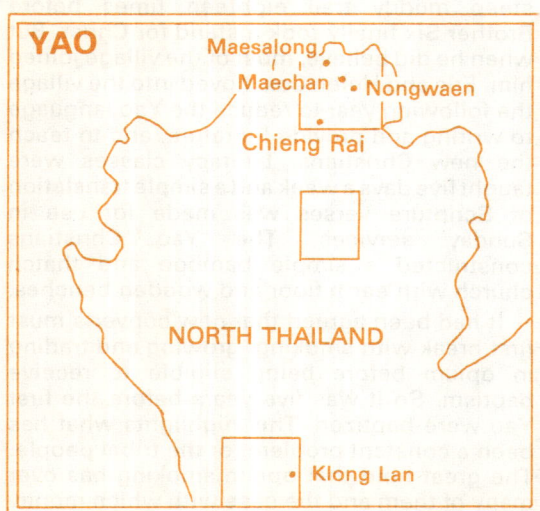

there are currently some 200 Christian households with about 150 baptized Christians and churches in 28 villages. But sad to say, few among the Yao seem to be gripped by the message of the Gospel or have caught the vision of living all-out for God. In some, money and position continue as the driving forces in their lives. Some still cling to old animistic beliefs alongside Christian truth and new believers follow the standards of older Christians. Little seems to be known in daily experience of the liberating, energizing power of the Holy Spirit.

One sign of encouragement is the church in the Khlong Lan area of Kamphengphet province. This is a resettlement area with Yao, Lisu and Hmong, Christians and non-Christians, who have moved from many parts of north Thailand. A church has been built there and is full most Sundays. Literacy classes are held nightly both for children and adults, with the result that many in this area can read and sales of literature have been encouraging. There is hope that a real advance will be made which in turn will spread throughout the Yao in Thailand.

QUESTIONS
1. The Yao are vigorous and hard-working, one would think they would become all-out Christians. But this is not so. What reasons can you see for the state of the Yao church?
2. Some of the professing Yao Christians continue to grow opium. What do you think is the result — in their own lives, in the church, and in the community?
3. Only 70 out of 150 baptized Christians can read. What do you think are the reasons for this? And what are the results in church services, young people's meetings and in the daily lives of these Christians? How would you encourage more to learn to read?

THE WHITE HMONG

Work among the White Hmong (formerly called Meo) began when Finnish Pentecostal missionaries living in the town of Lomsak in Petchaboon province noticed tribal people coming down from the nearby mountains to sell in the market. They approached OMF who sent Don Rulison and his Sgaw Karen helper to visit in the area for some six weeks. As a result nine families in the village of Namket burnt their demon altars. Ernie and Mertie Heimbach moved there in 1954 to begin learning the White Hmong language and to teach these families, some of whom stood

though others turned back. The first baptisms were a long time in coming and were fiercely contested. The village headman attended services for a year before he burnt his demon alter, but he died suddenly a week before he was to be baptized.

Some time later there was interest in the large village of Palm Leaf, twelve hours' walk north-west of Namket. The Rulisons moved there in 1958 and a small nucleus of families believed. Missionary nurses carried on the work, using medical work as a means of breaking down the suspicion and antagonism. During 1961 Roy and Gill Orpin had visited the village of Bitter Bamboo and found some response, but also great opposition; on his last trip to take in supplies before moving to live there, Roy was shot by Thai robbers. Hmong Christians visited him in hospital just before he died, and he exhorted them to preach the Gospel. One of them, Jahu, took this to heart and became a faithful witness, and in the next two or three years he saw eight families turn to the Lord. But to Jahu's great disappointment they slowly lost interest, and, despite his teaching, they turned back. He became discouraged, losing his hope that others would turn to the Lord.

Eventually most of the Christians from Namket moved to Cawca to find new fields, and Gill Orpin teamed up with Doris Whitelock and joined them. A translation of the New Testament into White Hmong had already been started, and now Doris concentrated on this task with Ying as her main helper. Later the two ladies moved across to Laos (where there are also large numbers of Hmong) to continue Bible translation while a missionary couple replaced them in Cawca. By now there were more than 20 families of Christians, with a church building and elders. A regular five-day Bible school took place with a visiting speaker from Laos. Most of the Christians were literate and hunger for the Word of God increased.

In spite of these encouragements, there were problems too. Hmong Christians witnessed well in their own villages but had shown little interest in going to other communities. (This may have been because of clan taboos — when making a visit Hmong will only enter a house of their own clan). Most of them had become Christians through medical work, which therefore played an important part in the missionaries' outreach. But one very disquieting feature was that nowhere had converts stood where there had not been a resident missionary — and out of 24 missionaries designated to the Hmong work, no less than 17 had left after fairly short periods. And nowhere had whole villages or even large groups turned to the Lord, as had happened in other tribes.

In 1969 Communist activity in the Pitsanuloke — Petchaboon mountains led to all the missionaries being evacuated and most of the Hmong Christians moving to the plains as refugees. The Cawca group fled to the Nong Say refugee camp, and the Palm Leaf and White Water Christians to the Nakonthai camp. Two years later these two groups resettled into one large village called the Fortress; by then there were about 30 families in the church, with Sing and three other elders as their leaders. Others fled to Phayao where a small refugee village was built, and six of the men were able to attend the Bible Training Centre.

These six graduated from Phayao in 1971 and each was encouraged to move to a new area as a farmer—church-planter. Nzoe moved to Now, a village in Lampang province where he had visited as a student. Before long 15 families had turned to the Lord and he

taught them faithfully and led them in witness. People in two other villages became Christians, and Nzoe's brother Simon moved up to help with the task of teaching.

On graduation Drew went out to the Chiang Khong area, where soon nine Hmong and two Yao families had turned to the Lord. Two years later missionary Dorothy Jones moved in to help Drew, and shortly afterwards the first baptisms were held. The first area believers' conference was attended by 24 Christians from four villages, and there are now over 90 believing families in this Chiang Khong area.

Around 1970 interest in the Gospel began to quicken in another area south-west of Chiang Mai. One family who had been reduced to poverty through spirit worship and sickness turned to the Lord; they later moved to Lime village and there Mr Nolan and his family believed too. Leona Bair went to live in Lime for several years to teach the Christians, and some eight families followed the Jesus way.

One of Mr Nolan's sons, Forest, later moved to the small village of Cone Va in the hills off the main road. A number of families there turned to the Lord, and Leona Bair has made visits in to teach them and hold mini-onferences. The great need is still the lack of local Hmong leaders.

Doris Whitelock has continued her work on Bible translation as well as a ministry among Hmong refugees from Laos. The New Testament was completed in 1975, and selections from the Old Testament is to be printed in the near future. Bible study notes, correspondence courses and a magazine are also produced in Hmong.

There are nearly a thousand professing Christians among the White Hmong scattered over north Thailand. The main concentration of leaders is in the Fortress, Turtle village and Elephant Grass village. In 1978 an annual seminar to train the leaders and elders of these scattered Christians was begun. The response and interest has been encouraging, as has been the report of what some of these men have begun to do in taking more responsibility in their villages. It is hoped to increase their skills in preaching, teaching and counselling; with new missionary reinforcements to give further instruction and pastoral care, the White Hmong church should advance.

QUESTIONS
1. What attracted the Hmong to become Christians? If you were a missionary to the Hmong, how would you plan your evangelistic outreach?
2. Imagine the effect on Jahu of hearing Roy Orpin's last works encouraging him to preach the Gospel. Why did Jahu stop? What keeps our vision fresh and bright? What dulls it?

THE BLUE HMONG

The first Christians among the Blue Hmong were Noah, Job, Vang Vu and Widow Sing, in Yellow Creek village. Missionaries began Bible translation and taught the Christians; but little outreach was done and after more than ten years there were still only 20 adult Christians among the Blue Hmong. Some of the young people lived at a very low moral standard and there was bickering in the group.

In 1969 Communist activity forced many Blue Hmong to leave the mountains and resettle in the plains, calling their village New Yellow Creek. Barbara Good and Barbara Hey moved in with the refugees to study the Blue Hmong language, and as their language ability increased they gave teaching, taught literacy and translated some Old Testament stories. In 1970 the New Yellow Creek church hosted the Hmong conference for both White and Blue Hmong Christians. At the time of the move Noah's son Mark and his family joined the White Hmong refugees at Phayao and attended the Bible Training Centre.

In the early 1970s Mark and his family moved to Huey San in Chiang Mai province, where missionaries and two Hmong girl graduates from Phayao had been working. During the next two years others in this and a nearby village believed. But the Hmong were not settled and a new area, Rock Village, was opened up; the two Barbaras with Mark and his family moved with them. Even in the new location there was strong pressure against the Christians. One promising young man named Ying turned back from the Lord as a result of sickness, death and pressure from relatives. Finally the Christians decided to move again, this time to Turtle village in Kamphaengphet province.

The two Barbaras and Mark had worked

closely together for four years. They translated large portions of the Old Testament and produced Theological Education by Extension (TEE) materials, travelling long distances every month to hold seminars with 62 scattered TEE students.

In July 1973 a large family turned to the Lord in Huey Yuam village in Maehongson province. The father proved to be a good leader and a keen evangelist, while one of the sons taught himself to read from a hymnbook by listening to the hymns on a cassette. Gradually others became interested both in Huey Yuam and in another village nine hours travel away. Cassette players and teaching tapes in Hmong were a tremendous help to the young believers when missionaries could only make occasional visits.

At present there are 700 Blue Hmong Christians of whom 230 are baptized. Nearly half of these are in the Kamphaengphet—Tak area; roughly 170 in the Pua area (for which OMF took over responsibility from an American mission in 1974); another 100 in Maehongson province and another 100 in Chiang Mai province.

QUESTIONS

1. *Missionaries to the tribes of North Thailand may have to live in a remote village, cut their own firewood for cooking, wash in a stream and grow their own vegetables. They may have to trek over mountains to visit, preach and teach, and be miles away from the nearest shops, post office or hospital. What special problems and temptations do you think they face as a result of this?*
2. *Much of the work among the Blue Hmong has been done by single lady missionaries. Yet among all the tribes, men are the leaders. How can ladies take the Gospel to the Hmong or teach them the faith? What special care do these lady missionaries need to take?*

THE KAREN

There are between one and a half and two million Karen in Burma, and some 200,000 more spill across into Thailand, making them the largest tribe in this country. They are located all along the Thai-Burma border, scattered in pockets in the lower mountains and in some places mingled among the rural Thai of the plains. Of the three main branches of the Karen there are slightly more Sgaw than Pwo in Thailand, but very few Red Karen.

There has been a Karen church in Burma since the days of Adoniram Judson. Sgaw Karen evangelists came over to Thailand in 1880 and some Karen were won to the Lord in Lampang province. In 1950 the American Baptist Mission was invited to help train leaders, and there are currently over 5,000 baptized Sgaw Karen in Thailand.

PWO KAREN

Traditionally far less responsive, the Pwo Karen were virtually unreached by the Gospel when OMF entered Thailand. They are basically animist but those in close contact with the Thai have also a strong veneer of folk-Buddhism. The first OMF advance to the Pwo Karen began in 1954, when workers trekked widely over the hills in Chiang Mai province, and Gospel Recordings in Pwo Karen were a great help. But little interest in the Gospel was shown. In the early '60s several Pwo Karen believed and were baptized, but in 1967 opium, envy and disobedience led to the break-up of the group.

A key event happened in 1970 when Mrs Dee Waters of Prosperity Fields refused to become a leader of spirit worship and opted to become a Christian instead. However, Phayao Bible Training Centre claimed missionaries Jim and Louise Morris for several years, and OMF almost gave up the Pwo Karen work as unresponsive. The New Tribes Mission began work in one area. But at the 1974 Field Conference it was decided not to give up the Pwo Karen work, but rather to make that year a Prayer Thrust for advance among them. The Morrises returned to Karen work and moved to Hot. Almost immediately the Lord began to answer prayer.

Some of the widows in Prosperity Fields had seen how the Lord had cared for Mrs Dee Waters. Although she did not feast the spirits she was able to grow rice and feed her family — and a number of times she was healed in answer to prayer. Several of these ladies began to join her on Sundays to listen to the cassette player. When the Morrises moved back to the area these women were ready to burn their demon things and turn to the Lord. Even Mrs Gahng, a leader of spirit worship, decided for Christ, despite the prediction that the spirit would seek revenge and all her family would die. In fact, a couple of months later, her bright 21-year-old daughter did die, probably of food poisoning. Yet she and other Christians stood fast.

The Lord was teaching the Karen that turning to Christ does not mean that one will never be sick or die. A heavenly hope was beginning to dawn among the new believers, and the motives of those desiring to turn were purified. Even so, it was obvious to all that the Christians were, on the whole, much healthier than before.

Since 1974 there has been a steady trickle of Pwo Karen turning to the Lord in the mountain area. Several have gone back in times of sickness, but some of these returned to the Lord at a later date. The Christian community grew from ten at the beginning of 1974 to 189 in mid-1975, and to 250 at the

present time, of which 42 are baptized. There are Christians in two villages on the plains and twelve in the mountains.

Four new lady workers have joined the Morrises, and the great task now is to lead the Pwo Karen Christians on to true discipleship and maturity in Christ.

QUESTIONS

1. From 1954 to 1974 there were hardly any Pwo Karen who became Christians. What changed this?
2. There are few Christians among the Pwo Karen who live on the plains, but a growing number in the mountain villages. Why do you think this is so?
3. Should Christians expect to be in better health than non-Christians? What do non-Christian tribesmen in North Thailand turn to when they are sick? — what about Christians? Can sickness and poor health have a divine purpose in our lives?

SGAW KAREN

Some relatives of Mrs Dee Waters lived in a mixed Pwo/Sgaw village, Sop Lan, located about 50 kilometres south of Prosperity Fields. In 1975 the influential Sgaw Karen headman of this village turned to Christ, just before the Morrises left for furlough. Taught by cassette tapes, a group survived a year without missionary visits. When the Morrises returned others wanted to believe — and most of these were Sgaw who did not understand Pwo. Who could follow up this potential movement to Christ? Missionaries to the Pwo had more than enough work to do. It was also important that work in both dialects should follow a similar pattern. So after consultation with other missions OMF opened this new field to the Sgaw as an extension of the Pwo work.

In 1978 Heinz and Christianne Mayer moved to Sop Lan followed quickly by Peter and Dianne McIvor. Both couples are learning the language with the help of a Sgaw Karen intern student from Phayao. A whole village of twenty households turned to Christ recently, plus some influential men in other places. There are now over a hundred in five villages believing. Several have broken with opium. The prospects for the future are bright indeed.

THE SHAN

The Shan people are not a tribe but a branch of the Thai race to which the Thai, Northern Thai and Lao also belong. There are many thousands of Shan in Burma, and the majority of those in Thailand live in the extreme northwest corner bordering on Burma. They are a complacent, self-satisfied group; ardent Buddhists, but with a great deal of animism mixed with it. Of all the work in North Thailand, that among the Shan has been the most disappointing. In the early days the workers trekked right across Maehongson province, preaching in homes and to groups. Medical work has been carried on by Dr and Mrs John Webb (experienced Shan workers who moved across from Burma) and by nurses and paramedics. Contact with young people has been maintained through youth meetings and English classes. Yet the response has been meagre and many of the earlier 'converts' reverted when the opposition of relatives became too strong.

Unlike the work in the tribes, Shan have become Christians as individuals rather than as whole families. This has made for weak witness, and constant opposition from unbelieving relatives has been the norm for

QUESTIONS
What passages of Scripture can you think of that refer to families (or clans or villages) becoming Christian? Are there dangers in whole groups turning to Christ, and how can these be overcome?

every one of the converts. In Shan families it is the mother who attends to the household shrine and who has the greatest influence in deciding whether the whole house becomes Christian. Eight Shan men are Christians but their wives do not follow them in their faith.

The whole Bible was available in the Shan language, translated by missionaries in Burma. But this is in Shan script, rather akin to Burmese writing, and in a different dialect of Shan, so in recent years a retranslation using Thai script has been started. Judy Crossman is spending some of her time on this task.

Although the work of the Kingdom among the Shan people has been slow and hard, with the devil fiercely contesting every inch of ground; and although there have been many disappointments and falling away from the faith, yet today God is advancing His Kingdom steadily and it is wonderful! In 1977 Dr John Webb was called to see a new leprosy patient, Mr Pooh, who lived in the fields just off the road. When Anna Cappon took over the leprosy treatments, she found him eager to be taught the Word of the Lord, and with regular teaching he and his family believed, and were baptized in August 1979. By that time his faith had become known in the neighbouring villages, and now Sunday services are held in his home, and four families in the vicinity want to become Christians. Mr Pooh's son-in-law in Fishfields village, away up towards the Burma border, is also a leprosy patient and he too became interested. Mr Pooh has visited them with Anna, and now fourteen adults there are talking of turning to Jesus! Much prayer is needed that, with regular Bible teaching both by missionaries and fellow-Christians and by cassettes, these and other seekers will cast off all that belongs to demons and experience new life in Jesus.

QUESTIONS

1. The whole Bible has been translated into Shan in Burma. Why is it not immediately useable among the Shan in Thailand?
2. Jesus taught His disciples not to persevere in unresponsive areas (Matthew 10.14, Luke 10.10-11). Does this 'shake-off-the-dust' principle apply to pockets of OMF work in Thailand? Have we ever considered it might apply to some Christian work in the west? How would you lead up to taking this very serious step? (Consider also the section about the Karen. Can you think of other relevant sections of this book?)

BIBLE TRAINING CENTRE PHAYAO

The need of a Bible school for some of the tribal Christians had been thought and prayed about for some years. In June 1965 John Davis began to look for a possible site, and that year also an inter-tribal leaders training school took place at Nong Waen Yao village. The following year this was held on the new site of the Bible Training Centre. Since then this has developed into a school with buildings for staff houses, dormitories, chapel, lecture rooms, library, dining room and kitchen. Pigs, cattle, vegetables and fruit trees are being developed. The 83 students at present in residence study for three years and spend one year as 'intern' in a church situation before graduation. There are six resident Thai staff and three missionaries as well as visiting teachers.

   The original aim of the Bible Training Centre was to cater for the training of leaders for the tribal churches. This has proved impracticable, and Phayao has swung to being a general Thai Bible School to which tribal people, with sufficient Thai language ability, also come to study. It now has its own Board independent of OMF control, and plans for the future include Thai staff in all executive posts. It is expected that missionaries will continue to serve on the staff and Board for some time to come.

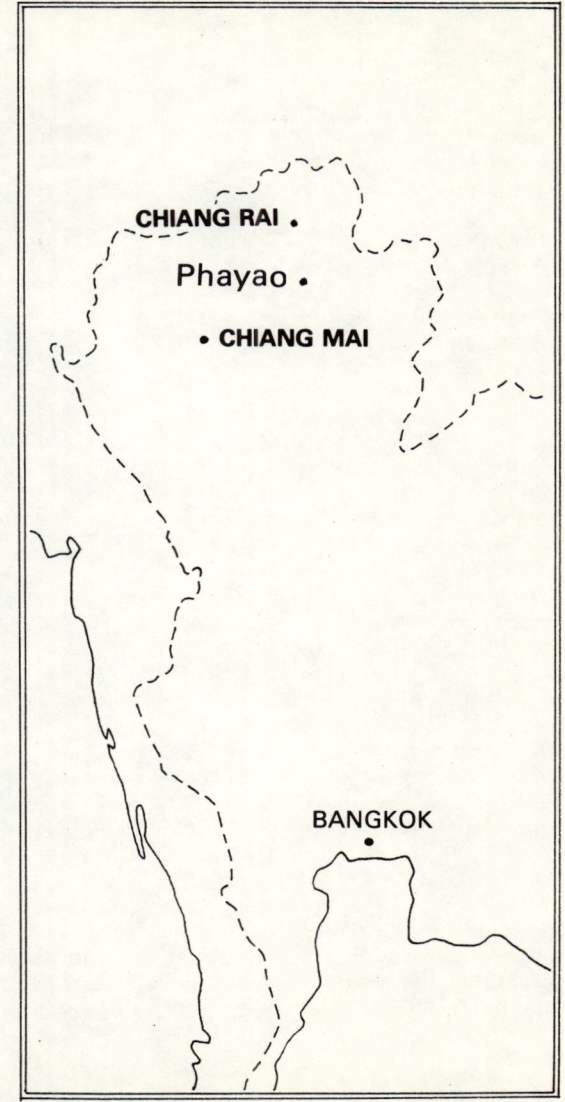

INTO THE FUTURE

As this chapter is being written a new decade has begun and beckons us on into the future. While our hearts are full of true thankfulness to the Lord for what He has accomplished in this land, it is to the future that we must apply ourselves. As always one is poised at the pivot point of past and future, in which yesterday's patterns and tomorrow's needs and demands converge on the present. For some the vistas of change excite and challenge the imagination, for others the security of the status quo can become a refuge behind which we hide. We need courage lest the past inhibit our ability to discern the new things which the Lord wants us to do, or lest the attraction of the novel unhinge us from the realities and responsibilities of our present commitments.

What then of the future? Several church leaders have said that the church has made more progress in the last five years than in the previous 150. Is this an exaggerated claim? Perhaps so, but it does indicate that the church is moving forward with a new momentum. During the last two years there has been a worldwide prayer thrust for breakthrough in Thailand. The desire has been to see the Lord Jesus Christ break through in power and glory to bring large numbers to a living faith and a real discipleship in the fellowship of His Church. We have to say that we have *not* seen a great turning to the Lord and a reviving in the Church, nor the outpouring of the Holy Spirit that we have longed for.

At the same time, there have been signs that the Lord has been answering prayer, and that when Thailand's church history comes to be written these years will be seen as a watershed in her growth. There has been a deepened sense of urgency on the part of many Christians, which is reflected in an increased desire for more evangelism and personal witnessing, and also in an increased burden for prayer. This emphasis on prayer is most significant. It is a recognition that the Church needs to look to God and is dependent upon Him for growth, and also that the future of a Thailand in which the Gospel can continue to be preached freely depends upon God. Another sign is the increased spirit of co-operation amongst Christians which is a joy to experience. Where numbers are small it is essential for Thai to cooperate to make any significant impact on society.

But perhaps what most clearly focuses the impression that there is a greater openness to the Gospel and responsiveness as a result of the prayer thrust is found in a recent survey of a cross-section of society in Bangkok. In answer to the question, 'Who is Jesus Christ?' 19% answered, 'He is the Son of God.' There is much to suggest that with the continually increasing numbers of Bible school students and trained full-time workers, the fruit of the prayer thrust for this land is yet to come.

What then of the future? Our original strategy, in response to the two compelling factors of the lostness of the lost and the shortness of the time, led us to spread our resources widely. Personnel were spread throughout Central Thailand, our resources poured into the sowing of the seed of the Word of God. Today those two factors, and others, are propelling us forward to new strategies. Originally there were few, if any, Christians in the areas where we were working. Now there are churches with leaders and national Christians to reach out in evangelism and teaching. Formerly we worked alone, now we work with the Church whether tribal or Thai. Our strategy has changed and must continue to do so.

In Thai society, the continuing drift from the rural areas towards the towns and the government's plans for investment in such towns compel us to reinforce our commitment to the towns rather than rural villages. The Central Thailand Field strategy for district towns has to be seen to be of the Lord against this backcloth. Our new work in Bangkapi in Bangkok and the need to press ahead with church planting in the burgeoning suburbs of this great city is part of this strategy to bring our resources to bear upon the towns. We can no longer afford to spread our personnel widely, and whereas traditionally we have seen it as our responsibility to spread the Gospel far and wide throughout the country, we can no longer think in these terms. The strategy for the 80's lies in missionary and national personnel working together as teams in which different gifts can be used to complement one another. By concentrating personnel in adjacent areas we can maintain continuity of work, and by concentrating in areas of responsiveness, focusing on district towns, we can bring our forces to bear in a deeper thrust within a more prescribed area. As one church leader has said, 'In order for churches to be able to grow on their own there has to be the discipling of leaders so that they may not only know what is in the Bible but know how to relate it to their everyday lives. So often missionaries are evangelising the next group but do not see to the discipling of the existing one.' So, in order to maintain the cutting edge of evangelism and at the same time disciple and train leaders, teams of workers need to be concentrated together in more limited and strategic areas.

In the churches with whom we work in North, Central and South Thailand and Bangkok, different churches and groups are at different stages of their development. Some are still at the pioneer stage, whilst others are functioning under national leadership and

reaching out to plant other churches. Whilst previously, in the pioneer work in which we have been involved, the initiative and leadership has been the responsibility of the OMF, the future holds a much greater emphasis upon national leadership. 'We see in the coming decade a great increase in the number of men being trained for the ministry, receiving Biblical education,' say Thai church leaders, 'so there are likely to be more, not less, national workers in the period ahead.' We can anticipate the expansion and upgrading of Bible schools, including the need to establish graduate level facilities in Biblical education and theology. The Church needs writers, theologians and commentators, as well as leaders, church planters and pastors. Whilst the missionary role continues in pioneer evangelism and grassroots church planting and in theological education in front-line service, the emphasis in the '80s must also be upon the training and establishing of national leaders. The decision to place our medical work at Manorom under national leadership at the end of this decade is a bold venture of faith and prayer, and one which will be a testimony to the Church in Thailand that we mean what we say in our desire to see the Lord's work firmly in the hands of national leaders.

In the area of mass communications, too, there is going to be change as new tools are available to spread the Gospel. The videotape project pioneered at Manorom and now in use also at Nongbua and Saiburi hospitals is an example of the way in which modern technology is being used to present the Gospel. This is not a substitute for the irreplaceable personal witness and testimony, but a tool for the spread of the Gospel, and can of course be used not only in evangelism but in teaching. The cassettophone has contributed significantly during this last decade to reaching isolated Christians and groups with teaching material. The possibilities for expanding this and other forms of technology remain a challenge for us in our overall goals of evangelism and training.

What of the future? Only the Lord knows the answer to this question. Shortness of time for missionary work in Thailand has been a recurrent theme ever since OMF came here 27 years ago. At the same time circumstances and events around us, world trends, economic and social stress leave little margin for comfort from the human point of view. Yet world events and world leaders are in the hands of God.

It has been no accident of history that Thailand, an uncolonized country and therefore enjoying an easy-going life and knowing little of the yoke of oppression, should see on her borders the consequences of totalitarianism. It is no accident of history either that spiritual blessing has often accompanied physical and material restrictions. Events in Cambodia both before and after the fall have challenged the Thai church not only to the possibilities of God visiting this country in blessing but to His doing so through straitened circumstances. Attitudes are changing. Easy-going and undiscerning tolerance are no longer appropriate to today's world. An earnestness not only about the faith but about life and death itself is stiffening the backbone of some of the Thai. Leadership there is, both of the older paternal type and those now emerging from graduate schools and Bible colleges, prepared to take life and the Lord Jesus Christ seriously in their desire to establish His Kingdom.

We have watched events in Indo-China with some dismay, fearful of the dismantling of all that has gone on before to build the Church of God. And through the fires of testing emerges the Church of God indestructible and

strengthened. Thailand still waits for breakthrough, when the Lord will visit His people and this country in unknown, unprecedented power and glory. Perhaps previously the people of God were not ready, not prepared, unconcerned. Surely that can not now be said. Barriers can be removed by the power of God and the forces of darkness, which for so long have held sway, can be destroyed.

The purpose of this book is to stir up interest in Thailand and in the growth of the Church here, slow though that may be. May we join with the people of God in Thailand in Isaiah's prayer, 'Oh that you would rend the heavens and come down; that the mountains would tremble before you. As when fire sets twigs ablaze and causes water to boil, come down to make your Name known to your enemies and cause the nations to quake before you.'

FOR FURTHER READING

Missionary Methods: St Paul's or Ours *Roland Allen* (World Dominion Press/Eerdmans) 1962

The World's Religions *J N D Anderson* (IVP) 1950

Chinese Churches in Thailand *Carl Blanford* (Suriyaban Press, Bangkok)

At Any Cost *Mertis Heimbach* (OMF) 1964

Ascent to the Tribes *Isobel Kuhn* (OMF/Moody Press) 1956

Mo Bradley and Thailand *Donald Lord* (Eerdmans) 1969

Paddy Field Hospital *Catherine Maddox* (OMF)

Status of Christianity Country Profile — Thailand (MARC, Monrovia) 1974

The Bridges of God *Donald McGavran* (Friendship Press) 1955

How Churches Grow *Donald McGavran*

Understanding Church Growth *Donald McGavran*

A Half Century among the Siamese and the Lao *Daniel McGilvary* (Revell) 1912

Thai Values and Behaviour Patterns *Robert Mole* (Charles E Tuttle, Toyko) 1973

Thailand, Its Peoples, Its Society, Its Culture, *Frank Moore* (HRAF Press) 1974

Roaring Lion *Robert Peterson* (OMF) 1968

Thai Peasant Personality *Herbert Phillips* (University of California Press) 1965

The New Trail *Otto Scheuzger* (OMF) 1963

Strategy to Multiply Rural Churches *Alex Smith* (OMF Publishers, Bangkok) 1977

Buddhism and the Spirit Cults in Northeast Thailand *S Tambiah* (Cambridge University Press) 1970

Little Things *Prajuab Thirabutana* (Collins/Fontant) 1971

Minka and Margaret *Phyllis Thompson* (OMF)

Missionary without Pretending *Anne Townsend* (Scripture Union)

History of Protestant Work in Thailand *Kenneth Wells* (Church of Christ in Thailand) 1958